1962

The Love That Lingered

THE BOOKS OF SALLIE LEE BELL —

THE LOVE
THAT LINGERED

by
SALLIE LEE BELL

ZONDERVAN PUBLISHING HOUSE
GRAND RAPIDS, MICHIGAN

The Love That Lingered

CHAPTER ONE

SHE WAS A PITIFUL LITTLE OBJECT when Warren first saw her, dirty face streaked with tears, tangled hair that gleamed red gold in the sun, a row of faint freckles across her short little nose. She reminded Warren of the pictures he had seen of the children on the streets in Oriental cities after the war, abandoned waifs with no homes, no parents and nowhere to go.

Warren was returning from the library and was riding slowly along on his bicycle. He was dreaming, as he so often did, of the day when he could enter law school and one day become a lawyer. He had a secret dream of one day sitting on the bench as judge. His grandfather had been a judge who had made a name for himself before Warren was born. His photograph in his robes stood on the mantel in the living room at the Lancaster home. Warren had often stood before it and wondered what his grandfather was like when he wasn't wearing his robes. He had often asked his father about him and Edwin Lancaster was always ready to talk to him about the grandfather he had never seen, for Edwin was very proud of his father and the record he had achieved as a judge.

Warren would have passed the forlorn, dirty little mite if he had not heard her sobbing and calling out in a tear-strangled little voice, "Mommy! Mommy! I'se hungry. Mommy, where is you? Where is you?"

When he reached her as she toddled along, stumbling from sheer weariness, he stopped and got off his bicycle. Then she turned and saw him. She stopped dead in her tracks and stared at him through her tears. She stuck one dirty little hand

7

in her eye and began to rub it, rubbing more dirt on her already dirty face.

Warren was afraid that she would try to run away from him, but she stood there rubbing her one eye and staring at him out of the other.

"What's the matter, little girl?" he asked sympathetically.

"I want my Mommy," the child cried, then began weeping again.

He had a tender heart for all small things and this mite was quite small. She couldn't be more than three and perhaps not that.

"Where is your Mommy?" he asked as he took hold of her grimy little hand and drew her to him.

To his surprise she didn't pull away and he was glad.

"Where is your Mommy?" he repeated.

"I don't know," and the tears flowed faster. "She just went away. I'se hungry and I can't find her."

"Where do you live?" Warren asked.

"I don't know. I'se lost," she wailed. "And I'se hungry."

"What's your name, honey?" he asked, drawing her closer.

"Babs," she said between sobs.

"Babs what?" he probed.

"Just Babs," she replied.

"What's your Mommy's name?" he asked hopefully, wondering how he could find the woman if he didn't know her name.

"Her is Babs too," she said.

This wasn't very helpful, but there was one thing he did know. The child was hungry and he knew that she would find a sympathetic helper in his mother. Perhaps later he could find out where the child lived and who she was.

"You come with me and I'll see that you get something to eat and then we'll try to find your Mommy," he said.

He was afraid that the child might refuse to go with him, but she brightened at the prospect of food and went with him willingly as he took her hand and led her to his bicycle. He put her in the luggage basket and rode slowly so as not to frighten her.

When he reached the gate of his home, he saw his little brother Bobby in the yard playing with his dog Towser. Towser barked joyfully when he saw Warren. Warren called to Bobby to open the gate and the little dog bounded toward Warren as he rode into the yard.

The child began to cry and threw her arms around Warren. "Take him away!" she cried in a high treble of fright. "He bites!"

"Don't be afraid," Warren said soothingly. "He's glad to see you. He wants to play with you."

She stopped crying but she still clung to him as he lifted her down from his bicycle. She wouldn't let him go and he stood there in a rather awkward position while Bobby stared at them with serious eyes. Bobby had just turned five and he bore his advanced age quite importantly.

"Where did you get that?" he asked, eyeing the mite with disapproving eyes.

"Don't ask questions. Just get Towser away so I can put her down," Warren said.

Bobby obeyed. He had great respect for Warren's fourteen years. He wished that he were fourteen. Then he'd be as big as Warren and he wouldn't always be hearing his mother saying, "Do as your big brother says."

He put the dog in the back yard and shut the gate, then returned with his question.

"Where'd you get her and what're you gonna do with her?" he demanded.

Bobby didn't like girls. They didn't like to play boys' games and this one was too dirty. He knew he wouldn't like her. He hoped that Warren wasn't planning to keep her. Life would never be the same if he did that. She would always be screaming every time Towser came near her. He'd have to keep his dog in the back yard out of her way. Storm clouds were evident on his horizon as he frowned and waited for the answer to his question.

"I found her on the street," Warren informed him. "She's lost and she's hungry. I'm gonna get Mom to give her something to eat."

Bobby trailed after the two as they went into the house. Babs had released her strangle hold on Warren's neck when the dog was safely behind the fence and she clung tightly to his hand as he led her inside. They went into the kitchen where his mother would most likely be just then.

When his mother saw them, she uttered an exclamation of surprise.

"Who is this and where did she come from?" she asked.

"I found her on the street," he said and then told her how he had found the child.

"I can't find out who she is," he said. "All she knows is that her name is Babs and that's her mother's name too. She said she was lost and hungry, so I brought her to you."

The child said nothing, but stared with avid eyes at the array of cookies on the table.

"Poor little thing," Mary Lancaster breathed.

She knelt down and drew the child to her. She smiled at her, but Babs stared at her and said nothing. Finally she said, "I'se hungry."

Her lip trembled and there came the threat of tears.

"Suppose we go and wash those tears away and then I'll fix you something to eat. How about that?"

Babs nodded and Mary led the child into the bathroom. When they returned to the two waiting boys, a transformation had taken place in the dirty little waif. With her tears washed away and her hair combed carefully, Warren saw that she was really pretty. She gave him a shy smile as he smiled down at her and he saw a dimple in one cheek. Her eyes, no longer smudged with tears and streaked with dirt, were bright blue and the tiny freckles across her short little nose didn't mar the clear whiteness of her baby skin.

Bobby continued to stare at her malevolently.

"Is she gonna stay here? Do we have to keep her?" he demanded.

"We'll keep her until we find out who she is and where she lives," his mother informed him. "In the meantime, let's see if we can find something she will like." She turned to Babs who was still eyeing the cookies longingly. "How about a cup of hot chocolate?" she asked. "Then you can have some of these cookies that I just baked."

"What's hot chocolate?" Babs asked doubtfully.

"Would you rather have a glass of milk?" Mary asked.

Babs nodded. "Me like it," she said, with her eyes still on the cookies.

Mary sat her on a chair upon some books and placed the milk and cookies before her. The child ate ravenously and downed a second glass of milk. Then she sat back and sighed contentedly.

"Poor little thing!" Mary murmured. "She must have been half starved. Tell me, little Babs," and she turned to the child with a smile, "did you have breakfast this morning?"

Babs shook her head. "Mommy never comed back. Me don't know where she is," and her lip trembled again.

"Don't worry," Mary soothed. "We'll find Mommy and you can tell her that you had a nice lunch. Wasn't that a nice lunch?"

Babs nodded and repeated, "Nice lunch." Then she clambered from the chair and went to Warren.

"Let's find Mommy," she said as she took his hand.

"Yes, let's look for her," Bobby agreed enthusiastically.

He didn't want his happy life to be upset by the addition of any female.

"Where shall we look?" Warren asked his mother. "I suppose I could go over to the project and ask, but if she were lost, she couldn't have come from there. She was too near it when I found her."

"We'll have to phone the police," his mother said. "We'll tell them that we have her and that we'll keep her until they find her mother. She'll be better off here than down there with a lot of men who might frighten her."

"O.K. Let's phone the police," Bobby hastened to interpose.

"What's the matter, boy?" Warren asked. "You seem mighty anxious to get rid of Babs. Why?"

"I don't want her around," Bobby stated. "She's afraid of Towser and she'll start screaming every time he tries to play with her. I'd have to keep him in the back yard and he don't like that."

"You need someone like her to keep you straight," Warren told him. "I'd like to keep the little tike. She's sort of got under my skin. She'd get used to Towser and you'd have a lot of fun with her."

Babs took hold of Warren's hand and looked at him with appealing eyes.

"You good to Babs. Me like you. Does you like me?" she asked with a smile and a wheedling tone in her voice.

Warren put his arm around her and said, "Sure, I like Babs

She's a little doll. How'd you like to stay here and be my little sister?"

Her face brightened as she exclaimed, "Fine! Don't look for Mommy. Me stay here wif you."

"Don't put such ideas in her head, Warren," his mother reproved. "We've got to find her mother. Something may have happened to her."

"Perhaps she's one of those creatures who go out and get drunk and forget that they have children who need them," Warren said.

Mary phoned the police and told them what had happened and before long an officer came out to interview her about the child. In the meantime Babs refused to leave Warren's side. He told her that he would have to study and he went to his room and sat at his desk. She followed him in, and though he tried to persuade her to go back to his mother, she shook her head and announced, "Me stay here wif you."

"If you stay here, you'll have to sit there and be quiet or I shall take you out and lock the door," he said firmly. "I've got to study and I can't have you talking. Do you understand?"

She nodded. "Me won't talk."

She sat down upon a little hassock nearby and cupped her chin in her hand while she fixed her deep blue eyes upon him adoringly.

He was rather disconcerted, but he opened his book and tried to read, though it was hard for him to concentrate with that little figure sitting so quietly with her eyes fastened upon him.

Presently, to his relief, his mother came and asked him to talk to the officer. When they had told him every detail, he said he had better take the child with him while they tried to contact the mother, but Mary asked if they might keep her until the mother was found. She explained that the child would be better satisfied with them and that they would take good care of her. When he finally left, Warren asked his mother to take the child off his hands so that he might study and she took care of Babs until time to prepare for dinner.

Presently Mr. Lancaster came in and found Babs happily occupied with one of Bobby's outgrown toys which he had reluctantly consented for her to use.

CHAPTER TWO

EDWIN LANCASTER WAS A FINE LOOKING MAN in his late thirties. His son Warren had inherited his good looks. With the boy's thick brown hair, level brows, firm chin and dark eyes, he looked much like photos of his father at his own age. Lancaster was the head of a prosperous business and he had been able to provide his family with every comfort. They had been just a little disappointed when Bobby was born, because he wasn't a girl, for they had both wanted a girl, but of course they lavished love upon Bobby and he never knew that he was a disappointment to them. There was such a difference in the ages of the two boys that Bobby, as the baby of the family, had been spoiled more, perhaps, than was good for him.

It had been a disappointment to Edwin's father that he had chosen to go into business instead of following in his footsteps in the practice of law, so when Warren began to show an intense interest in law, his father encouraged him in it. He felt, somehow, that if Warren became a lawyer, it would make up for his own failure to satisfy *his* father's ambition for him.

When he came in and saw Babs there, he stood watching her for a moment while his eyes lighted with pleasure. She looked at him and smiled. She was happy now and she could smile at every one. She seemed to have forgotten all about her mother and about the fact that she was lost. She was interested in the toy and she held it up for his inspection.

"Bobby gived it to me," she said proudly.

"That's fine," he said and knelt down beside her.

She was a charming little mite, in spite of a dirty dress

13

that was much too large. Her baby face would have served
as a model for one of Raphael's cherubs.

"What's your name, little one?" he asked.

"Babs," she informed him.

"I'm so glad you came to visit us," he told her.

"Me not visit," she told him. "Me stay right here. Me like
it here."

Mary came in just then and greeted him. She told him how
Babs happened to be there.

"I'm like Warren," she said. "I wish we could keep her.
She's just what we've wanted all this time, a little girl. It would
be just perfect if she were really ours."

"H'm. I wonder how long it will take them to find her
mother," Edwin remarked.

"Some mother she must be," Warren commented as he came
into the room and greeted his father. "To go off and leave that
poor little thing to wander around and get lost and to be almost starved. You should have seen her eat."

Bobby came in noisily, banging doors and ignoring his
mother's reproving look. His father took him in his arms and
gave him a hug. Bobby eyed Babs with a frown.

"Ain't you found her mother yet?" he asked disgustedly.

"It would be good if we never found her," Warren told him.

"Don't say that!" Bobby cried.

"What's the matter, son? Wouldn't you like to have a little
sister?" his father asked.

"No, I wouldn't!" Bobby said emphatically. "She'd be
a lot of trouble. She's afraid of Towser. I got to keep him
locked in the back yard while she's here and he's been howl-
ing because he don't like to be cooped up like that."

When dinner was ready and Babs was set at the table
upon a pile of books, she stared in silence as Edwin asked the
blessing. When Mary served her plate, she began to eat like
a little savage and Mary knew that the child had had no training at all in table manners. She tied a napkin about Bab's
neck so that she wouldn't get her dress any dirtier and she
tried gently to show her how to eat.

She wondered if the child's mother was worrying about
her and it worried her when she thought of what she might
be suffering. She wondered if that mother had tried to contact
the police.

After dinner Edwin phoned the police and asked them if they had heard anything about the missing child. He wondered why, if the mother were not hurt in some accident, she hadn't contacted the police. They said that though they had sent out radio calls, there had been no response and they were beginning to think that if the mother weren't injured in some hospital, that she might have disappeared. Just another case of abandonment.

Not long after dinner Babs was already half asleep, for the excitement of the day had been too much for her. Mary got out a pair of Bobby's outgrown pajamas and then she remembered the bed that Bobby had occupied until recently. She had laid it aside to give to the Salvation Army, but now she was glad that she hadn't given it away. She and Edwin got it down from the attic and put it in their bedroom.

She undressed Babs, but when she took her into the bathroom and prepared her bath, the child objected strenuously to being bathed. Only after much persuasion could she induce Babs to let her put her into the tub. When the trying ordeal was over and she was clean and sparkling in her clean pajamas, she ran out into the living room where Warren sat with his father.

She climbed upon his knee and put her arms around him as she gurgled, "Babs is nice and clean. Me like you lots. Tell me goodnight."

He put his arms around her and held her close for a moment, then he kissed her on her forehead.

"You're a clean little angel," he said, giving her a smile. "Now go to sleep and have pleasant dreams."

"You like me?" she asked, still clinging to him. "Me love you."

"Sure I do. Now scat," and he put her down.

"You've surely made a hit with her, son," Edwin remarked as the child went to the room where Mary was waiting.

Warren flushed self-consciously.

"It's just because I found her and brought her here," he explained.

"She'll never forget you if she lives to be a hundred. This will stick in her mind no matter what she may be called upon to endure when she grows up and has to face the world."

"I'll never forget her, either," Warren replied.

Just before Mary put Babs to bed, she knelt down beside her bed and pulled the child down beside her.

"Let's talk to God before you go to sleep," she said.

"Who's God?" the child asked as she knelt obediently beside Mary.

"He's the One who made you and who loves you more than anyone else could ever love you. Don't you pray to Him before you go to bed?" she asked, though she knew by the child's question that she didn't have the least idea what prayer was.

Babs shook her head. "Me don't know God."

"Let's talk to Him. I want you to know Him. Let's ask Him to take care of you tonight and to make you a good girl tomorrow and help us find your Mommy," Mary suggested.

"No! Don't find Mommy," Babs said with a vigorous shake of her head. "Me stay here. Me don't want God to help us."

Mary couldn't repress a smile, though her heart ached for the child. She feared the worst for her, that her mother was one of those creatures who deserted their children when poverty made them too much of a burden.

"We'll just ask God to make you a good girl and to make you a happy little girl. Only good little girls are really happy," she added. "Now close your eyes and bow your head and repeat what I say."

Babs obeyed, repeating the simple words that Mary told her to say.

When they rose from their knees, Mary lifted her into the bed and then bent down and kissed her on her cheek.

"Now go to sleep and have happy dreams," she said.

Babs reached up and put her arms around Mary's neck.

"Me love you," she said. "You good to Babs. You don't fuss wid me. I so glad I find you."

"Bless you," Mary whispered as she released her and let her lie down again. "I'm glad you did find me. And I love you, little one."

As she turned out the light and closed the door, her eyes were misty. When she joined the family in the living room, her husband gave her a smile.

"I'm afraid that poor little thing has been terribly neglected," she remarked as she sat beside him on the couch. "She doesn't even know who God is and I'm sure she never prayed before. She didn't want me to ask Him to help find her mother. She said she wanted to stay here. I feel that it would be a tragedy if we did find her mother."

"Now don't say that," Edwin said. "That mother may be having hysterics because she can't find her child. Just imagine how you'd feel if she was yours and you had lost her."

"I never would have left her alone. I wish she *were* mine," she added with a sigh.

"Well, I sure don't," Bobby announced from across the room. "I want you to find her mother and get her out of here. I don't want her to stay here."

The next morning Babs was awake before anyone else. She climbed out of bed and slipped into the living room, then opened the door so that she could see what was going on outside. Towser saw her and came bounding to her, hoping to be allowed inside. She uttered a frightened cry and shut the door with a bang.

The cry wakened Mary and she got up and hurried out to see what had happened.

"Dat dog," Babs explained. "He wanted to bite me."

"You mustn't be afraid of Towser," Mary said. "And you mustn't be running around like this before anyone else gets up. You must be a good girl and stay in bed until time to get up for breakfast. After breakfast we'll see that you and Towser make friends. You'll have fun playing with him if you're not afraid of him."

She took Babs back and dressed her. She made a mental note that if they had to keep her a day longer, she would have to have a clean dress. She couldn't go around in that dirty, ill fitting dress any longer.

When the family was seated at the table, Edwin asked Warren to return thanks. When he had finished, Babs piped up, "Me talked to God too. Last night," she informed him.

She turned an inquiring eye upon Mary.

"Did God hear me when me talked to Him?" she asked.

"Of course, dear," Mary assured her. "God always hears everything we say."

"How do you know?" the child persisted.

"Because His Word tells us that He does," Mary replied, realizing that her answer wasn't very enlightening to the child.

"What's His Word?" Babs asked.

"Aw, be quiet!" Bobby cried. "You ask too many questions. Eat your breakfast."

"Bobby!" Mary cried reprovingly. "I'm surprised at you. That's no way to talk to her. She could never ask any more questions than you used to ask and still do. *You* be quiet and eat your breakfast."

She turned to Babs who was looking at Bobby with a grieved expression upon her baby face and said, "Let's wait until after breakfast and then we can talk and you can ask all the questions you want to."

Babs obediently ate in silence while the others talked casually during the meal.

After breakfast Edwin left for town and Warren prepared to leave for school. Anxious to get started on that law course, he was taking a summer course, trying to skip a grade.

"Take me wif you," Babs begged when she saw that he was leaving.

"I can't, honey," he said. "You stay here with Mom and Bobby and be a good girl until I get back."

"Den will you play wif me?" she asked.

"Perhaps," he conceded.

She sidled up to him and took one of his hands and looked at him with anxious eyes.

"You still like me?" she asked.

"Sure I do. I like you lots," he assured her with a smile.

She raised her face and puckered her lips for a kiss. When he held back self-conscious and embarrassed while Bobby looked on with a frown, she said, "Den kiss me. Your Mommy kissed me last night. Me liked it."

He bent down and gave her a hasty kiss, then left her standing there watching him as he rode out of sight.

Mary had stood watching in the doorway and there was a tender smile upon her face as she came into the room. She was proud of her firstborn and his tenderness toward this little waif touched her. It made her doubly proud of him. Not many boys of his age would bother with a persistent little tike as he had done.

Bobby went outside and called to Towser and they began to romp upon the lawn. Babs saw Mary and went to her.

"Who's gonna play wid me?" she asked.

"Would you like to play with Bobby?" Mary asked.

"He don't like me and I'se afraid of dat dog," Babs said with a disconsolate note in her voice.

"I'm sure he'll like you if you make friends with Towser," Mary told her. "Suppose we go out and make friends with him right now."

"But he'll bite me," Babs objected, holding back when Mary opened the door.

"No, he won't, so don't be afraid of him. He's a nice, friendly little dog and he likes to play with everyone. Come on and let's make friends with him."

Towser saw them coming and ran to Mary and began to jump up and down, pawing her. Babs hung back and watched with frightened eyes. Presently Mary took her hand and rubbed it over the dog's silky coat while the little animal wriggled happily under her caress.

"See, he likes you," Mary told her. "Now you pet him yourself."

The child did so and Towser jumped up and down, pawing her and trying to lick her hand. For a moment Babs stood in petrified silence while her eyes dilated with fright, but as she became convinced that Towser wanted to be friends, she burst into a gleeful laugh and let him lick her face.

"He likes me!" she cried. "He likes me. He don't want to bite me."

"Of course he likes you," Mary assured her. "Now you and Bobby play with him. Get Towser's ball, Bobby, and you and Babs play with him."

"Do I have to?" Bobby asked with a disgusted glance at his mother.

"If you want to please me, you will," she told him, then she left them and went into the house.

Bobby reluctantly obeyed his mother, but he didn't try to hide his displeasure. Babs didn't seem to notice and she entered gleefully into the game of ball, throwing it while she watched Towser go after it and bring it back.

After a while Bobby's ill humor passed and they played together happily. As Mary looked out now and then and saw them, a tender smile flitted across her lips. She wished that she could keep this little waif, for she had already fallen in love with the child. She wondered where that mother was and what she must be enduring if she knew that her child was lost. Perhaps the woman had gone out on a drunken spree and didn't even know that her child wasn't at home where she had left her. So many of these cases had been in the papers. Perhaps this was just another of the same kind.

When Warren came home from school Babs ran noisily to meet him with Towser following at her heels. She threw her arms about him and held up her face for his kiss.

He kissed her hurriedly, then asked, "Have you been a good girl today?" .

"Yes — and Towser likes me. He won't bite me," she told him.

Bobby joined them and Warren noticed that his belligerent expression was absent.

"Have you two been having fun?" he asked.

"Yes," Bobby conceded. "She ain't so bad. She likes to play ball. I guess she'll do for a while."

"Have they heard anything about her mother?" Warren asked.

Bobby shrugged his shoulders and shook his head.

Edwin asked the same question when he came home, but they had heard nothing. The police said they had found no clue as to the child's mother.

When Babs had been put to bed, Mary altered the dress so that it would fit her better, then washed it. The next morning Babs was delighted to see the dress all clean and starched and that it fit her as if it had been made for her. Mary's heart went out to her as she surveyed herself in the mirror. The eternal feminine in her was conscious of the change in her appearance.

"Me looks pretty," Babs remarked, then she ran to Mary and held up her lips for a kiss. "You good to me. I love you lots," she said with a bright smile. "Better than my Mommy," she added.

Mary held her in her arms for a moment while the tears misted her eyes.

"I love you lots, little one," she said.

It was the first time Babs had mentioned her mother since the time she had said she didn't want them to look for her. Mary knew if they didn't find the mother soon, the child might forget her completely. Surely her life with her mother was not all that it should have been or she wouldn't be so well satisfied

away from her. Even a three-year-old would miss her mother
and be homesick for her if her life had been a happy one.

The next morning they finally got word from the police.
The child's mother had been located in the morgue. The un-
identified body had been picked up literally in the gutter the
day that Babs had wandered from home. An autopsy revealed
that she was an alcoholic and that death was from natural
causes. When it had finally been identified by a neighbor, she
said that the child had been left alone many times while the
mother was off on a drunken spree.

"We must keep her," Mary said when they received the
news. "Let's find out what legal steps we would have to take
to adopt her."

Edwin was as willing to adopt the child as Mary was and
he went to his lawyer's office to find out just what they should
do in order to adopt her. The lawyer told him that they would
first have to make an effort to find any possible relative who
would claim the child, then there would be a lot of red tape
that would have to be processed before they could finally adopt
her. In the meantime, he made arrangement so that they could
have custody of Babs until everything was cleared up.

Warren knew the facts, but Bobby was not told anything
except that Babs' mother was dead. He was cautioned not to
say anything about her in Babs' presence. The quicker she forgot her mother, the better it would be for her. They didn't want
Bobby to know the tragic details. They felt that it would be
better if he never knew.

The next day Mary took Babs to town and bought her the
clothes she needed and Babs was as proud of her new outfit
as if she were years older. She smiled and strutted before the
mirror as they tried on each dress and she insisted upon trying
on her pajamas, much to the amusement of the salesgirls watching her.

Mary gave her a dresser drawer to put her clothes in and
the child was as careful of them as if they were priceless,
fragile things.

She turned happily to Mary while her eyes sparkled.

"Babs got lots of things now," she said. "Me gonna throw
that old dress away. I'se tired of looking at it."

"We'll do that very thing," Mary agreed.

She left Babs at home while she went to the room in one

of the cheaper tenements where the child had lived, to see if there was anything belonging to them that might be saved for her, but there was nothing that Mary would want in her home. There was only the barest necessities in furniture and it was dirty and worn. The few clothes that had belonged to the mother were much worn and nothing was clean. She didn't see anything that might have fitted Babs except one other dirty dress that was too large for her.

Her heart ached for the child when she saw what a drab, unhappy life she must have lived. It was a wonder that the little tike was as good as she was. There must be something in her that had withstood the ugliness and drabness of her life. No wonder she didn't want to find her mother after she had had a taste of decent living. Mary hoped that they would be able to keep her and legally adopt her, for she knew that if she had to give her up it would tear at her heart. She already felt that Babs was her very own, almost as if God had sent her to take the place of the little girl they had never had.

CHAPTER THREE

MARY WAITED IMPATIENTLY while the effort was being made to find any possible relatives of Babs. If she had to give up the child, she wanted to have it over with as soon as possible, for every day that passed made the child dearer and the thought of parting with her harder to bear.

Babs became as much a part of the family as if she had been born into it. She called Mary "Mommy" as Bobby did. She seemed to have forgotten her own mother, for she never mentioned her and since no one ever talked of her past life in her presence, Mary felt that she had forgotten that life completely. She hoped that she had.

When night came and she was tired from playing and was sleepy, she climbed into Mary's lap and cuddled there until it was time for her to be put to bed. Mary's heart ached as she thought of the possibility of Babs being taken from her. It would be like giving up her own child.

Babs knelt obediently by her bed and repeated the little prayer that Mary had taught her, but after her first curiosity about God, she asked no more questions. Mary usually told a Bible story to Bobby before he got too sleepy and then read a short passage from the Bible. After Babs came, she had Bobby with her before Babs was put to bed, so that the child could listen with Bobby. She was interested in the stories and listened attentively, but she didn't display any interest when Mary tried to teach Bobby the application. She realized that Babs might be too young to understand, but she hoped that when she grew older, she would display more interest. Mary

23

had pursued this course with Warren and was happy in the knowledge that she had been able to lead him to the Lord when he was a little fellow. She rejoiced that as he grew older, he also grew in grace and the knowledge of the Word.

After his first resentment over her, Bobby accepted Babs and they played together happily. Babs was so delighted that Bobby accepted her that she agreed to all of his plans for games or anything that he might suggest for their amusement. She imitated everything that he did and she followed him around as faithfully as Towser did. This inflated the small boy's ego tremendously. Babs soon adored him and tried to follow suit in anything he attempted to do.

She even tried to climb a small tree which Bobby had climbed and built a crude little tree house. She got up just a little way and then slipped and fell, spraining her ankle so that she couldn't walk for several days. She cried for Bobby when he left her to go out to play and Mary took her out and let her sit and watch him.

Mary noticed one thing that touched her deeply. Though Babs adored Bobby and never wanted to be out of his sight, whenever her feelings were hurt or she was in the doldrums about something, she would invariably go to Warren, climb upon his knee and put her head on his shoulder, while she waited for some comforting word from him. It was usually something that Bobby had done or said in a fit of temper when things didn't go right in their play.

Warren was always able to comfort her and restore her good humor. He was never impatient with her, no matter how busy he was with his lessons or absorbed in some interesting book. Mary marveled at the boy's patience, for it was unusual in a boy so young. She didn't realize that Warren loved Babs as much as she did, though perhaps in a different way. It was a strange way which the boy didn't try to analyze.

Though his friends at school were already making dates with girls, he had never been much interested in them. He had many friends among them, for he was not only good looking, but full of fun and was popular with everyone who knew him. But he was interested in only one thing, to get to work on that law course and fulfill his ambition. Dates could come later.

When he was in school and often when he sat up late studying, the picture of a baby face would come before him and a tender smile would flit across his face. She had already carved a place in his heart which no one else would ever occupy, young as he was.

When the court finally gave the Lancasters notice that the search for the child's relatives had been abandoned and that they were free to begin adoption proceedings, there was joy in the hearts of all four of them. Even Bobby rejoiced, for he had at last acknowledged that it was nice to have a little girl in the family to play with — as long as she played the way he wanted her to.

The proceedings didn't take as long as they feared it would, so that before the year was ended, Babs was legally a part of the family. Mary thought it would be best for her to understand from the beginning that she was adopted, so that if anything came up in the future, it would be no shock to her for her to know the truth.

When Bobby started to school in the fall, Babs cried because she couldn't go with him. Mary tried to explain to her that she wasn't old enough to enter kindergarten, but she refused to be consoled. When Warren came home, she flew to him and insisted upon being taken upon his knee while she poured forth her grievance. He tried to console her but he wasn't succeeeding very well, for she kept saying, "What is I gonna do all by myself?"

Finally he hit upon a suggestion that helped to revive her spirits. He told her that he would make a ladder so that she could climb up to the tree house and have it all for her own while Bobby was away and that he would help her to make a little garden around the base of the tree. The suggestion appealed to her and she was once more in better spirits.

Edwin had a room added to the side of their bedroom, so that she could have a room of her own. She was so delighted to know that she would have a room of her very own that she hovered around the carpenters and chattered with them while they worked. Her grief over Bobby's absence was temporarily forgotten.

The little room was fitted with dainty furniture and ruffled curtains and her eyes glowed with pride when Mary let her see it for the first time after the carpentry work was finished. She stood wide-eyed and with lips parted, then she flew to Mary and put her arms around Mary's knees and cried," "It's wunnerful, wunnerful! And I love you for givin' it to me. You so good to me. Why?"

"Because I love you, for you're my own little girl," Mary told her.

"But I not your real little girl," the child replied. "You not my real Mommy."

Mary was surprised, for she thought that the child had forgotten her past.

"I am now, honey," Mary stated. "And you're my own little girl. You've been adopted, so you're just as much my own as Bobby and Warren."

"Where is my other Mommy?" she asked.

"Do you want your other Mommy?" Mary asked anxiously.

"No! No! No!" Babs cried emphatically. "She not love me like you. I was hungry an' afraid. But you love me and I ain't hungry no more. She went off and left me," and her eyes became dark with the memory. "Where did she go?"

"She went to another world, honey," Mary told her. "Maybe she knows that you're happy with me because I love you so much."

"And she ain't ever comin' back for me?" Babs asked anxiously.

"No, never. You're going to be with us and be my little girl."

"I'se glad she ain't ever comin' back," Babs murmured as she clung to Mary's hand while she surveyed the room.

Mary took her in her arms and they went into the living room where they sat and talked for a little while, then Mary went into the kitchen while Babs went outside to play with Towser.

The dog seemed to know when it was time for Bobby to come home and he would trot to the front gate and stand looking down the street expectantly. Babs followed him and watched with him. This made Bobby feel very important, though he tried not to show her how it pleased him to have her there waiting for him.

When her room was finished, she insisted upon escorting him proudly to view it.

"Ain't it just wunnerful?" she asked eagerly.

"Yeah," he replied without enthusiasm and she was disappointed because he didn't show any real interest.

"Don't you like it?" she asked as her spirits drooped.

"Sure I do," he said, realizing that she expected him to admire it. "It's beautiful."

Later on she took Warren in to show it to him and his enthusiastic remarks brought a gleeful laugh as she held his hand and listened to what he said. As usual, he hadn't disappointed her and she was happy.

CHAPTER FOUR

WHEN BABS WAS OLD ENOUGH FOR KINDERGARTEN, Mary took her and introduced her to the teacher. While other children were crying and clinging to their mothers, she stood by Mary's side and looked eagerly about her.

"Where's Bobby?" she finally asked.

They parted at the front door and she expected him to join them. It never occurred to her that she wouldn't be with him.

"He's gone to his class," Mary told her.

"Then I want to be in that class," she stated emphatically.

"But you're too little to be in that class," Mary explained. "You'll have to grow up fast so that you can catch up with him."

"I don't want to go to this school if I can't be with him," she declared.

It took patience and persuasion on Mary's part to make the little girl understand that if she didn't keep on in this class that she'd never be able to be with Bobby and that Bobby would be ashamed of her if she grew up and never went to school. Reluctantly she consented to stay when Mary left and before long she was enjoying the games and the instruction which was opening up a new world to her eager mind.

When she came home and the family gathered around the table for dinner, she chattered about all that had happened at school. She felt her importance, for now she didn't have to sit and listen to Warren and Bobby tell of their school happenings. She had affairs of her own to tell and she made the most of them, to the amusement of the others.

She expressed her scorn of the cry babies who wouldn't join

in the play and she related with enthusiasm several scuffles she had gotten into with little fellows who tried to take her toy away or push her out of place when they were marching.

"She's sure going to look out for herself," Warren remarked.

"You mustn't quarrel and fight," Mary warned. "Good little girls don't do those things."

"Then I'm not a good little girl," Babs retorted. "I'll be good when they're good, but they were bad first."

Warren laughed and Mary couldn't repress a smile. She felt that she was going to have a difficult time with this child from the slums, a much more difficult time than she had had with Warren. He had been so easily led, but this little child had a spirit of rebellion and she wondered where it would lead her.

Mary was concerned about Bobby as he grew older. When he was a small child and had sat by her side when she told him stories and read from the Bible, he listened with interest, but as he grew older she could see a growing indifference to spiritual things. She had tried to lead him to the Lord as she led Warren, but she knew that she had failed. She didn't want to force him or use undue persuasion, for she knew that this would not produce the result she hoped and prayed for.

By the time Babs left kindergarten and entered grade school, she was old enough to realize that she could never catch up with Bobby, but she did her best to make good grades so that he would be proud of her. She felt her importance when she took home her first report. She had seen Warren and Bobby hand theirs to their father and saw his pleased look when they had made good grades. She thrilled at his praise of her when she gave him her report.

She was determined that her family should be proud of her. She was able to skip a grade and she stood at the head of her class when the term ended.

She followed Bobby in his indifference to spiritual matters, soon outgrowing the nightly story telling and Bible reading. Though she went to church and Sunday school obediently with the family as Bobby did, she didn't display any interest in what she heard or studied. Mary felt that it was Bobby's indifference that was the stumbling block, but there was nothing she could do about it but pray.

By the time Babs was in high school, Warren had finished

his law course and had started the practice of law. He took Babs with him when he had his office furnished and she was all enthusiasm. She was so proud of him, now that he was a full-fledged lawyer.

"I just can't believe it," she remarked, "but somehow I wonder if I really like it. It makes me feel that you're growing away from me. You'll be so busy with all your cases that I'll never be able to sit on your knee and tell you all my troubles."

He looked down at her, for she was quite small for her age, at her lovely face with the sparkle she had always had even when she was a little thing, the red gold hair, the deep blue eyes, the rosebud mouth and pert little nose, and his heart beat with an ache. He couldn't remember when his boyish love for the little waif had changed into the love of a man for the one girl in his life, but it had been there all through his years at college, even before she had been old enough to know what love really was.

He doubted that she really knew now. She had always followed Bobby adoringly and still did, but he wondered if it was the same kind of love that he bore for her. He would have to wait patiently until she was older. But by then, perhaps she would feel that he was too old for her and she would never know the pain in his heart every time he looked at her and longed for her, yet feared to give her a hint of how he felt. If she didn't love him, it would make their relationship unbearable.

He gave her a slow smile and said, "Don't you think you're getting to be a young lady and too big to sit on an old man's knee?"

She stared at him seriously.

"Does that mean that you're tired of having me sit on your knee?" she asked in hurt tone. "I never thought I was bothering you. I'm sorry if I have."

He drew her to him and put his arm around her.

"Of course I'm not tired of having you sit there," he assured her. "I love it. But I just realized that you're growing up and that makes me feel very old."

"But you're not old. You're young and you're wonderful," and her expressive eyes spoke volumes. "Ever since that day you found me, you've been almost like God to me. I've come to you with all my troubles rather than go to Mom, for I adored you. I felt that I could find comfort in your arms and sitting on your knee that I never could find anywhere else, but I never thought that I might be worrying you. I suppose I just took you for granted, believing that my woes were just as important to you as they were to me. I never thought how you might be feeling or that I might be worrying you."

He drew her closer and held her while his heart beat faster with her nearness.

"I'm a stupid old blunderbuss," he said. "Just forget what I said. I've loved every minute of your trust in me and I've never been too busy to listen to your troubles or to try to make you happy again when Bobby hurt you or something else troubled you. You're my very own little sister and I've always thanked God for the day I found you. You'll always be the sweetest part of my life so I'll feel hurt if you don't keep on coming to me and I'll never be too busy to have you tell me what's on your heart."

She reached up and kissed him on his cheek, something she had rarely done as she grew older, and it sent the blood pounding through his veins.

"You're such a dear," she breathed, "and how I do love you. Next to Bobby, I love you best of all."

"Just keep on loving me," he said as he released her.

He knew that the childish adoration that she had for Bobby was maturing into something deeper, even though as yet she didn't seem to realize it. He couldn't help but feel a pang of jealousy. He wished that he were Bobby's age. Then there might be a chance that he could win her love from Bobby before she became aware of what she felt for him.

He uttered a sigh as she left him and he began to review a case that was coming up; but he found it hard to concentrate upon his work.

It was true that Babs still loved Bobby with the childish adoration that she had had for him from the first, but she was beginning to be jealous of his attentions to other girls at school. When there was a party in the gym or in one of the homes of the pupils, Bobby spread his attentions to all of the girls. He had a sparkling personality, just as Babs had, and he loved people. He was very popular, and he enjoyed his popularity to the fullest.

Babs was also popular, for her beauty had grown as she

grew older and she had many admirers among the boys in Bobby's age group. She could have had their attention and their friendship, but she ignored their attempts to date her. She had eyes only for Bobby and when she saw him with other girls, having a wonderful time while they played games or danced, she was miserable.

The fact that both of them went to parties where there was dancing, and that they danced themselves, was a source of deep grief to Mary. She debated whether it would be wiser to forbid them to go to these affairs or let them alone until they were convicted that they were wrong. She prayed earnestly for guidance and she and her husband discussed it often.

"It would do little good for you to forbid them to do these things," he said. "They're at that rebellious age when they would not only feel that you were being too harsh with them, but they would perhaps do the things we wish they wouldn't do, on the sly, and that would be worse, for it would be doubly wrong for them."

"I suppose you're right," she sighed, "but it is so hard to see how indifferent they are to spiritual things. I wonder where I've failed."

"You haven't failed," he assured her. "You've done everything in your power to give them the right instruction and to lead them to the Lord. If they're rebellious, it's part of the sign of the times, for we're living in a rebellious age, when the spirit of rebellion is taking over, not only in the older ones but the young ones as well."

"I know, but I don't want to see that spirit manifest in my own two. I want them to know the Lord while they're still young enough not to be tainted by the world's sin. I wanted them to be saved from the world and not have to be saved out of it."

"We'll just have to wait and leave it with the Lord. You've taught them the right way, you've prayed about them and with them, and you've wept over them, so the rest must be in God's hands. We'll just keep on praying and believing that in the end God will answer our prayers."

"I blame Bobby for Bab's indifference and waywardness," Mary said. "She's followed him and attempted to imitate him in everything he did from the very first. She adores him and still tries to follow his lead. If he yielded his life to the Lord, I'm sure that she would do the same."

"Don't blame Bobby for that," he argued. "Remember that everyone is accountable to God for himself. Babs has had the same teaching that Bobby had and she stands alone in her guilt, if she refuses to accept the Lord. Bobby may be a stumbling block, but that doesn't excuse her."

"That's true, but I still feel that if Bobby would take a stand so would she."

"Maybe it will be the other way around," he said with a smile as he put his arm around her. "Maybe Babs will take her stand and will be the means of leading him to the Lord."

She tried to act upon Edwin's suggestion and leave it in the hands of the Lord, but she found it impossible. One night Babs and Bobby came in unusually late, breaking the rules. They were not allowed to stay out after midnight and this night they had come in well after that.

The next day Mary spoke to Babs just after breakfast. Bobby had to leave for an early class. She led Babs into the living room.

"Sit down, dear," she said. "I want to talk to you."

Babs felt guilty. She thought she knew what was coming.

"You came home very late last night," Mary began. "Have you forgotten what your father and I told you and Bobby when you went out on dates?"

"We did forget last night," Babs admitted. "But Mom, we were having such a good time that we just couldn't help it."

"Where did you go after the party?" Mary asked. "I know it didn't last that long."

"We all drove out to Nick's barbecue house," she said.

"There's a dance band there, isn't there?" Mary probed.

"Yes," Babs reluctantly admitted.

"And you and Bobby danced."

Babs nodded.

"Nick doesn't serve just cokes. He also serves beer and other stronger drinks," Mary remarked with a sickening sensation in her heart.

"Yes, he does, but honestly, Mom, Bobby and I don't drink. We had cokes. Some of the boys in the crowd had other drinks but we never took anything but cokes."

"Thank God for that," Mary sighed. "Babs dear, I don't

want to lay down the law to you and Bobby, but I shall insist that you don't drink anything stronger than cokes and I insist that you obey our rule about the time you come in. Also, I don't want you going to places like Nick's. Both of you are too young to be turned loose without any restrictions, so until you are old enough or strong enough to be turned loose with our trust, you must obey the rules. I shall tell Bobby just what I've told you."

"I'll try, Mom," Babs said penitently. "I'm sorry we disobeyed. I never want to hurt you for I love you so very much."

Mary took the girl in her arms and murmured, "I love you very much, too. You've been God's answer to our prayers and I've known such joy in having you, but you're breaking my heart, darling, by the way you and Bobby are living. You seem to have forgotten everything I ever taught you about the Lord. You're getting farther and farther away from Him and I can't stand to see you doing that. Why don't you surrender your life to the Lord? You'll be so much happier if you would do that. I would be so much happier if you would."

"Oh Mom, just let us wait a few more years," Babs begged. "While we're so young, let us have a little pleasure. We would have to give up so much fun if we became Christians. We're having so much fun now and there's really no harm in it. Give us a little more time and I know that Bobby and I will both be what you want us to be."

"That's just the thing that grieves me, Babs," Mary said. "You think that you can go ahead and do what you please for as long as you want to, until the bloom of youth has withered, then you think that you can turn over a wasted life to the Lord and let Him have what is left of it. You can't do that, Babs. It doesn't work that way. God doesn't want a wasted life. He wants a life that can be used for Him. If you would just believe that the only true joy is to be found in Him, you wouldn't be so stubbornly rebellious. You would do what I've tried to persuade you to do, turn your life over to Him while He is calling you. When you have had your fun, it may be too late, for you can only come to Him when He is ready to receive you. You'll have to come in His time, not in your own."

"Mom! Please don't beg me," Babs pleaded. "I just can't do what you ask. Not now, at least. Give me just a little more time and everything will be what you want it to be."

"Bobby is keeping you from yielding your life to the Lord," Mary stated. "If you would surrender, then perhaps he would and you could both be happy in Him together."

"I want to be whatever Bobby wants me to be," Babs admitted. "I don't want to be separated from him."

"You may live to regret that some day," Mary told her, sick at heart and realizing that it was useless to continue the conversation any longer.

As she watched Babs leave for school, she wondered what the future would be. She would have to leave it in the hands of the Lord.

CHAPTER FIVE

IT WAS BABS' SIXTEENTH BIRTHDAY. Since the family couldn't get any accurate information about her real age or birthday, they had given her a day that they called her birthday. It was the day that Warren had found her.

Babs had accepted it, never realizing that it was a problematical date.

This was to be something special. She had always had a little party on her birthday and Bobby had always been there, joining in the games and lording it over the other children when they were little and enjoying himself immensely when they grew older with the evidence of Babs' worship.

This party was to be something different. Mary had invited Babs' friends to a dinner party in a private dining room at one of the better restaurants. There would be games and music afterwards.

Babs, who was old enough now to insist upon being called Barbara by everyone except her family, was thrilled at the prospect. Mary had gone with her to buy a dress and she was beautiful in it. She grew more excited as the day drew nearer.

"You really should wear a tux," she told Bobby. "You would be a knock-out in one and I'd be so proud of you."

"Sorry, sis, but I won't be going to your dinner party," he said.

Her face and her eyes were filled with hurt surprise.

"Not going!" she cried. "What do you mean, you're not going?"

"Just what I said. I've got another date. Had it before I remembered about your birthday. Besides, Babs, that dinner party will be kid stuff. I've outgrown all that balloon blowing and those silly little hats and kid games."

"Since when did you get so old?" she asked, not wanting him to see how hurt she was.

"Since I got to be almost nineteen," he informed her loftily.

"But we've always done things together and it didn't seem to make any difference about our ages. Why this sudden change?"

"I told you, honey. I made this date before I knew about the party and I forgot about your birthday. I'm sorry, but I can't break it. You'll be having such a good time that you won't miss me. I'll send you flowers and a big surprise and that'll be better than having me there looking bored and wishing that I was out with the fellows having a big time."

"I don't want your flowers or any big surprise, if you won't be there," she retorted while she struggled to keep back the tears. "You didn't used to be bored at my parties. You always took over and got a big kick out of them."

"That was when I was a kid," he told her. "I've grown up in this last year. I don't enjoy kid stuff any more. Sorry if you're disappointed in me, but I'll try to make it up to you in some other way."

"You needn't bother," she said as she turned away and left him.

At dinner that evening everyone noticed that Babs had lost her exuberance and that she seemed depressed. They wondered, all except Bob, what had happened that had caused such gloom when she had been bubbling over with such excitement.

"I think you should get a new suit for the party, Bob," his mother remarked.

Bob's face reddened and his eyes fell as he said in a halting voice, "I'm not going to the party. I have another date."

"Why Bob!" Mary exclaimed. "How could you do such a thing? You know that Babs expects you to be there."

"I told her I couldn't come," he explained lamely. "I'm sorry. I just forgot the day when I made the date."

"Then you can break the date," she stated firmly. "I won't let you disappoint her like that."

"I can't break the date, Mom. I just can't break it."

"But I insist that you do," Mary said severely.

"Don't bother about it, Mom," Babs said. "I wouldn't want

him to come. He's not that important and I wouldn't want him to be bored by having to attend a kids' party. He's such a man now that he would be bored, so he told me. Will you please excuse me?"

"Don't you want any dessert?" Mary asked. "It's your favorite."

"I couldn't eat any more," Babs told her as she rose from the table. "I'm not hungry."

Mary turned to Bob and looked at him with grave, disapproving eyes.

"I'm terribly disappointed in you," she said. "You know how you have hurt her. She looks to you to share everything that gives her joy. You've always been willing to do that. Why did you do this?"

"Mom! Can't you understand? I'm almost grown and Babs is still just a kid. I have other interests. I can't go along with her tagging after me or me tagging along with her for the rest of my life."

"You couldn't find any better companionship, I'm sure. Besides, can't you ever think of anything but yourself? Can't you be willing to make a sacrifice sometime to give someone else happiness? I've seen this selfishness in you when you were a little fellow, but I thought you would outgrow it. Instead, it has grown within you, in spite of all that I tried to teach you."

"Oh, Mom, stop preaching or you'll spoil my appetite."

"I'd like to do more than spoil your appetite," she retorted.

He finished the meal in sullen silence and conversation, after a few remarks between the others, finally ceased. When Bob finished his hastily consumed dessert, he asked to be excused and left the house. His father had wisely kept silent during his mother's rebuke.

"I think he should have been compelled to break that date," he said. "He's been running around quite too much lately. He's fast getting out of hand. The crowd that he goes with come from wealthy families and I don't like it. He'll be getting ideas far beyond him and it may lead to trouble."

"I can't forbid him to do things like I did when he was a child," Mary argued. "As he says, he's almost grown and he feels that he's a man already. I don't want him to defy me. That would be disastrous. I'm praying that he will be what I

long for him to be, what I've prayed that he would be, ever
since he was born."

"I only hope that the Lord answers your prayer before
I agree to take him into the firm," Edwin replied with a sigh.

He was so proud of Warren and so disappointed that Bob
was not following in his brother's footsteps. He had hoped that
Babs would lead him along the right path, but instead, she
had been more willing to follow him than to lead him.

"Babs is so terribly hurt and disappointed in Bob," Warren said. "She adores him and he's let her down. It will take
a long time for her to get over this, even though, after all, it's
such a little thing."

When Warren went to his room he heard the sound of sobs
coming from the den as he passed the open door. He stopped
and saw Babs sitting in a forlorn little heap on the couch,
weeping. She was muffling her sobs with her handkerchief. He
stood there a moment looking at her and his heart ached with
pity for her and with longing for the love that she was throwing
away on Bob. He went in and sat down beside her and took
her in his arms. She laid her head against his breast and sobbed
more bitterly as she felt his arms enfold her.

He laid his cheek against her rumpled hair and whispered
words of comfort to her.

"Don't take it so hard, little one," he murmured as he stroked
her hair. "There are so many more important things in life
to cry about than one boy's thoughtlessness over one little party.
There will be other parties and Bob will be there. I'm sure he's
sorry that he made you unhappy. He loves his little sister
but he's just thoughtless and selfish."

"If he loved me he'd want to be with me like I want to be
with him," she said brokenly between sobs which she was trying
to repress.

"You know he does love you just as I love you, as we all
do," he said, trying to reassure her.

"I don't want him to love me like the rest of you do," she
said. "That's not the way I love him. I love you with all my
heart," she told him, looking at him through wet eyes, "and
I'd die if I didn't have you to love me and hold me in your
arms and comfort me when I'm in trouble, but that's not the
way I love Bob. That's not the way I've always loved him.
He's someone special, but I'm beginning to see that I'm not

someone special to him. I'm just a kid sister who, after all, isn't his sister. I don't suppose I'll ever be anything to him," and she began to cry softly again as she clung to him.

He bent down and kissed her wet cheek. "Don't give up hope," he advised. "He's in the growing stage of becoming a man. When you're a little older, he'll begin to see what a lovely young lady you are. But remember, little Babs, that you'll always be someone very special to old brother Warren. My shoulder will always be ready for you to weep on and my arms will always be ready to hold you when you need me."

"How wonderful you are!" she exclaimed as she raised her head and gave him a tremulous smile. "What would I do without you? Oh, I do love you! So much!"

She raised her head and kissed him impulsively upon his lips.

He held her there for a moment while his lips answered her kiss, while joy surged through him. She had never done that since she was a little tike climbing all over him and pouring out her childish love.

"It's good to know that, Babs dear," he said as he released her, trying not to let her see just what that kiss had meant to him. "Just remember that I'll never change."

She felt rather breathless after that kiss, for she knew that he had held her there. There was something which puzzled her and made her wonder. Never before had there been anything like it between them.

"I wish that I could believe that Bobby would never change, but he has already," she said, though her thoughts were in a whirl and she was not really thinking of Bob.

She was trying to explain to herself what had happened to her when her lips had met his. She realized that she was no longer a child and that Warren was not really her brother. The thrill she had felt as his lips met hers had not come from a brotherly kiss and it puzzled her.

Warren sensed this and he regretted his weakness. He was ashamed of himself for giving way, even for that little moment, to the longing he had for her.

"Just have patience and I'm sure that one day you'll see that Bob has changed for the better. Mom's prayers will follow both of you and if it is God's will, you'll one day be happy in the love you want him to have for you," he told her. Then he rose to leave her.

After he left, she sat wondering and still puzzled and suddenly realizing that she was not so heartbroken as she had been before he came.

CHAPTER SIX

BREAKFAST THE NEXT MORNING was a rather silent meal. They listened while Edwin read from the Bible and then offered thanks. The passage that Edwin chose had Babs in mind. It was a chapter from Luke in which the Lord had been discussing forgiveness. When Peter asked how many times one should forgive someone who had trespassed against him, suggesting seven times, Jesus answered, "Until seventy times seven."

Babs knew that he had chosen that passage for her benefit and she resented it. She wasn't in the humor for a sermon and she gave Bob a scornful look while Edwin was reading. He turned away from her wrathful glance.

The three others carried on a desultory conversation while Babs ate in silence and Bob looked guilty and morose. As soon as the meal was finished, Babs went to her room. Bob was about to leave when Warren detained him.

"Come into my room. I want to talk to you," he said.

"What about?" Bob asked belligerently. "If it's about that party, I don't want to discuss it. I've said all I'm going to."

"We'll see. Come on. I won't keep you long," and Warren led the way to his room.

"I don't have to tell you how you've hurt Babs," he began when they were inside.

"No. I've been told already," Bob retorted.

"Perhaps you didn't realize how much it meant to her to have you there at her first real formal party," Warren continued. "Perhaps you don't realize, though you ought to, how much you mean to her, how she's always adored you from the very first when you and she played with Towser. Remember how she cried when the dog died?"

A smile flitted across Bob's face as he said, "Yes, I remember. She cried because she saw how I grieved over him. I guess she loved him as much as I did."

"She loved him because he belonged to you and she cried because she knew how his death hurt you. You should treasure that love she has for you, Bob. It isn't often that a child keeps that love as she grows older. That childish love is often forgotten as a person grows older and that love turns to someone else. Hers has never changed. Try not to hurt her or disappoint her. If you do, it will kill something within her that may embitter her for the rest of her life."

"You mean that she's really in love with me?" Bob asked in a worried voice. "I wouldn't want that to happen!"

"Perhaps just a young girl's infatuation," Warren offered. "She's at the age when most girls get crushes on someone and perhaps her crush right now is on you. She may get over it, but be kind to her and don't let her down. Just go on being her pal and try not to be bothered if she demands more of your time and presence than you're willing to give her. She'll be growing up fast from now on and perhaps her demands won't be so trying. She'll find other interests."

"I'm sorry about the party," Bob confessed. "I meant to tell her so this morning, but she gave me the brush-off. I didn't have the nerve to try."

"Suppose you give her a surprise at her party," Warren suggested.

"I told her that I planned to do that, but she said she didn't want anything from me. Besides, I'll need most of my allowance for my date," he confessed.

"Would you mind telling me what that date is that's so important?" Warren asked.

Bob hesitated a moment, then said reluctantly, "A bunch of us are going on blind dates. Tom Ewell's sister is a good looker. She's in love with some boy but her mother won't let her go out with him unless Tom goes with them on a double date. She promised Tom that if he and our bunch would go with her and her boy friend on blind dates, she'd have some good looking girls for each of us. I promised Tom that I would go."

"Where is this important date going to be?" Warren asked.

"We're all going to a showboat on the river at the downtown wharf."

"And there'll be dancing afterwards, of course," Warren remarked.

"Yes, but it'll be a decent place and there won't be any rough stuff there," Bob offered defensively.

"And this is important enough to make you hurt Babs and make her more unhappy than she's ever been," Warren commented with a shake of his head.

"It is important. If I don't go, Tom and the others would be angry, because I'll break up the party. This girl I'm to go with might be someone important and she might be just the one I'd fall for."

"Don't you know that you're hurting Mom and breaking her heart?" Warren asked seriously. "She's tried so hard to lead you in the right way, yet you're turning your back on the Lord and making it harder for you to ever accept salvation. I've heard her praying for you while she wept over you when you were out later than you should be. And it's breaking my heart to, Bob, for I know where you're headed and it shouldn't be."

"Please don't start preaching!" Bob exclaimed angrily. "You said something about giving Babs a surprise. Let's get that over with and let me get out of here."

"I thought that if you would send her an orchid and then have a lovely gift for her at the party, it might help make her happy as she should be on this special occasion."

"An orchid!" Bob exclaimed. "Where do you think I'm going to get the money for that? My allowance won't stand the strain."

"I'll attend to that, if you agree," Warren told him. "Just write a little note and sign it on this card," and he pulled one out of the desk drawer. "I'll have it enclosed with the package and have your name in the box with the orchid."

"Sure I'll agree," Bob said with a relieved sigh. "That's swell of you. You like the kid, don't you?" he added.

"Sure I do," Warren replied. "We all love her. We've loved her ever since the day I brought her here. Since I did that, I sort of feel responsible for her. She has no one else but us and I don't want her ever to feel that she can't depend upon us."

"Thanks again, fella. I'll try to make it up to her in some way. I do love her, but sometimes she can be annoying."

He wrote the note that Warren had suggested and then waved a good-by to his brother as he left the room in a much more cheerful frame of mind.

Warren stood looking down at the note with a thoughtful frown wrinkling his brow. He was relieved to know that Bob was not in love with Babs, though he should have known it before. If the boy had been in love, he would have been at that party. Perhaps, as he had suggested to Bob, she would outgrow her childish infatuation and then he might have hope of winning that love for himself. But, he sighed, he was so much older than she was. How could he ever tell her how much he loved her? She would never think of him having a love like that. To her, he was just a refuge in time of storm, someone who gave her the comfort she needed, not someone who wanted her for his wife. The knowledge would appall her and might drive her further from him.

There was a look of sadness in his eyes as he left his room and went to his office.

Until the day of her party Babs continued to eye Bob with studied indifference, an indifference she was far from feeling. He was very handsome and her heart beat faster when she looked at him surreptitiously, but there was an ache in her heart with that fast beating. She knew that he didn't love her in the way she loved him and it hurt deeply. She had not been conscious until lately that her childish adoration had merged into a more mature love. She had been happy in the revelation, believing that one day Bob would wake up to the fact that his feeling for her had also changed.

When he had calmly stated that he had forgotten her birthday and refused to break the date he had made for that night, she knew that he didn't love her. Perhaps he never would love her. He would always look upon her as his kid sister and some day he would fall in love with some other girl. Then her heart would really be broken.

Bob didn't try to talk to her. He thought it best to wait until she received the surprise on her birthday. Then he would try to make amends and ask for her forgiveness. He had enjoyed being pals with her and he didn't want to destroy the peace in the family by letting anything come between them. It would hurt everyone if that happened.

When her birthday came and she opened the packages

from her family, her eyes glowed with happiness over their love and thoughtfulness. In every package there was something that she had expressed a desire for at some time during the year and it touched her to know her every wish had been granted, as far as possible, ever since she had become a part of the family.

Her eyes filled with tears as she went to each one of them and gave them a kiss and murmured her thanks. She gave Warren a hug and kissed him on his cheek.

"You're the best big brother a girl ever had and I love you heaps and heaps," she told him.

It had been her favorite expression when she had given him her childish affection in the days past.

He smiled and replied, "I love you heaps and heaps."

There was nothing from Bob and he wasn't present when the packages were opened. No one said anything, but Babs was more hurt than ever, though she tried not to show the hurt.

Late that evening when she was dressing, the door bell rang and a messenger was there with a box from a florist. Mary took it and smiled as she handed it to Babs.

"Oh, what a beauty!" Babs exclaimed as she took out the lovely orchid. "I never dreamed of getting anything like this. It'll be beautiful on my dress, for it just matches the color scheme. Is it from Dad?"

"Read the card and see," Mary advised.

She read the card and her eyes opened wide.

"It's from Bob!" she exclaimed. "Where on earth did he get the money to buy an expensive thing like this? I know he's usually broke before the end of the month."

"What's the old saying? 'Don't look a gift horse in the mouth,'" Mary remarked. "Just wear it and be thankful."

Bab's eyes clouded. "It's lovely and I do thank him for it, but, like I told him, I'd rather have him there than all the flowers in the garden. Even wearing this flower won't make me happy at the party because he won't be there."

Mary's eyes were thoughtful. Bab's words made her think seriously. Babs was fast becoming a woman. She seemed older at times than her years. Could it be possible that she was in love with Bob, not as the little shadow who followed him everywhere and hung upon his every word and let him lord it over her, just contented to be near him and to meet his approval?

Would it make either of them happy? Would it draw either of them to the Lord? They were both going down the road to destruction together. If they should ever marry, would they surrender their hearts to the Lord or would they still go on the road each had chosen?

Babs was sparkling and excited and appeared not to be thinking about Bob and her disappointment over him as they drove to the hotel, but her thoughts were still on him. She wished that he could have seen her in her new dress, made more attractive with the orchid on her shoulder. She had surveyed herself in the mirror when she had dressed and her shining eyes told her that the image she saw in that mirror was lovely.

The dinner party was all that she could possibly have desired. Everyone ate with the hearty appetite of youth while gay chatter and jokes brought peals of laughter.

Just before the dessert was served, the lights were turned out and a waiter stood in the doorway with a cake bearing sixteen lighted candles, while other waiters sang "Happy Birthday," with the young people joining in.

When the lights were turned on again, Babs saw that there was a box decorated with gay ribbon and with a flower on top, placed beside her plate. After she had blown out all the candles and the cake was being served, she opened the box and gave an exclamation. Inside there was a little clock radio that she had admired once in a shop window. She saw the card with the note and she read it while tears filled her eyes.

"Please forgive me for not being at your party. I'm truly sorry that I forgot when I made this other date, but you know I never could remember dates. Mom always had to remind me and she forgot it this time. I promise to do better next time, honest. Your ever loving Bob."

She held the radio up while the others admired it and smiled happily as she announced, "From my brother Bob."

When the party finally ended and a tired but happy group went their several ways, Babs got in the car with her mother.

"This was such a wonderful party," she sighed as she laid her head on her mother's shoulder. "How can I ever thank you for being such a wonderful mother to a poor waif like me?"

"Don't ever say that, Babs," Mary reproved her. "I wish you would forget that past and think of yourself as being what you are, our very own child, just as surely as if you were our own flesh and blood. We think of you as that and we love you as if you were, so that's the way you must always feel."

"I love you as much as if you were my real mother, though I know you're not," Babs said seriously. "Sometimes the memory of the past comes back to me, of the days when I was so little and so hungry all the time. For a long time I did seem to forget it completely, but lately, the memory comes to me. It's like a bad dream. I wish I could forget it."

"I wish so too," Mary replied.

"I shall never stop loving you," and she kissed Mary on her cheek. "Thanks for the lovely party, the presents and everything."

A tear splashed on Mary's cheek from her own eyes. She was remembering the little waif, so dirty and pitifully hungry and of the time when she had put her thin little arms around her neck and had told her that she loved her.

When they reached home, Babs said she wanted to sit up and wait for Bob, so she sat on the living room couch and waited.

It was after midnight when he finally opened the door and tiptoed in stealthily. When he saw Babs sitting on the couch he uttered a gasp of surprise. She had been nodding, but wakened the instant he entered.

"What are you doing up at this time of night?" he asked.

"I was waiting to thank you for the lovely orchid and the present," she said as she gave him a smile.

She stood up and faced him, letting him see her loveliness in the light of the lamp nearby.

"See how beautiful it is?" she asked with a smile. "Everyone admired it and that made me very happy."

He came to her and took her hands and said, "Then I'm forgiven?"

"Yes, but I missed you terribly," she admitted. "Somehow it wasn't the same without you."

Her beauty struck him forcibly for the first time. He realized as she stood close to him, that she was no longer just a little girl, but that she had grown up. She was beautiful and desirable.

"If I'm forgiven, let's kiss and make up," he said as he drew her to him.

She didn't have time to refuse if she had wanted to, for he held her and kissed her swiftly, then reluctantly let her go.

"You're beautiful, much more beautiful than any other girl I know," he remarked as she stood breathlessly near him. "To think I have such a girl for a sister! I'll have to guard you to keep the wolves from trying to capture you and take you from me."

His words killed the joy she had felt at the touch of his lips. Though she thrilled at their touch, it meant nothing to him. To him she was still just a kid sister, no matter how beautiful he might think she was.

"Good night and thanks again for the lovely flower and the gift," she said as she turned away and went to her room.

He stood looking after her. He felt guilty over the knowledge that the gifts were not really his, but Warren's. The touch of her lips had thrilled him. He had never kissed her before that he could remember. She was beautiful and she was desirable. He had a grave, thoughtful light in his eyes as he went to his room. She was much prettier than the girl he had held in his arms on the dance floor and had kissed in the darkness of the dimly lighted room. She was much more desirable, in her untouched, girlish loveliness, than this other girl. What a pity she wasn't in that other girl's place, with money and class and position in the social world.

As Babs shut the door and began to undress, there were tears in her eyes. She unpinned the flower and held it to her cheek, then kissed the delicate petals. She didn't want to put it in the refrigerator. She would press it and keep it as a souvenir of this night. It would remind her of that first kiss that Bob, her adored Bobby, had ever given her. Even though it might have meant little to him, it meant much to her.

As she drifted off to sleep, the memory of that other kiss, the one Warren had given her, came to her. She remembered the clinging pressure of his lips before he released her. There was such a difference in those two kisses. There was something more than just a big brother touch in that other kiss, only the careless caress in Bob's.

As she finally lost consciousness, she was wishing that somehow those two kisses could be exchanged, that the warmth and tenderness from Warren's kiss could be transferred to Bob's. How wonderful that would be!

CHAPTER SEVEN

BABS SEEMED HAPPY AGAIN and Bob seemed in a more cheerful mood, and Mary surmised that they were friends once more. She had spent a restless night thinking of the situation between Babs and Bob. She hoped that Bob, in his thoughtlessness and selfishness, wouldn't hurt Babs, for she felt sure that he was not in love with her. She hoped and prayed that there would be no heartache to either of them.

She had given up thinking of Warren, for he seemed destined to continue in single blessedness. She had asked him once about his lack of interest in girls. He was so engrossed in his work that he never took time out to enjoy their company. He knew a number of attractive young women in his age group, but he had never become interested in any of them. Mary was sorry that he was so unconcerned about them. She wanted him to be married, for she felt that that would make him happy. She most emphatically did not believe in single blessedness. She felt that is was intended for a man to have a wife and a family, and that without this union, life would be incomplete. Loneliness would eventually come and there would be no one who really belonged, to help bear that loneliness.

She asked him one day about this when he seemed more preoccupied than usual. He had been reading, but he put the book down and sat there with it upon his knee. He was usually in his room, bending over his desk or deep in the study of some law book.

"Would I interrupt you if I sat here beside you?" she asked.

"Of course not," he said and as she sat beside him he put

his arm around her. "It isn't often that we get a chance to talk together. You're either busy about the house or else Dad claims your attention."

"And you're either deep in those books or working on some case. You never take time out to relax or enjoy life a little."

"I've taken time out this evening," he said with a smile. "I'm trying to read this silly novel. I thought it might relax me, but it bores me."

"You were thinking about something that made you sad," she remarked. "I don't often see that expression on your face. Would you mind telling me what you were thinking about, or is it none of my business?"

"I wouldn't say that," he replied with a smile. "I was thinking about Babs. She's getting to be quite a young lady and such a pretty one. I was thinking that it might not be long before she finds someone who might take her away from us and then we surely would be lonely without her. She's been like a ray of sunshine in this house ever since I brought her home."

"I believe she's in love with Bob," Mary said. "I saw that when she talked to me before her party."

"I think she is, but it may be just a passing infatuation, the first girlish crush. She's at the age when she's in love with love itself."

"I don't believe Bob loves her. I wish he would. I'd rather see those two married than for either of them to marry someone who might not be congenial with us. I'd hate to see the family broken up, but I do want them to get married. That's the way it should be, for complete happiness in life."

"Complete happiness only if the two are suited to each other and if they are both living for God, and neither of those two are," Warren said. "That's one thing I was thinking of. I was wishing that there was some way that I could make Babs see how she is wasting her life by refusing to let God take control of it."

"I've tried time and time again to talk to both of them but neither of them will listen. It only seems to irritate them."

"That's the experience I've had," Warren said. "All we can do is to pray that they will see how wrong they are before it's to late."

"Why don't you go out and have a little fun, son?" Mary

asked. "You know a lot of girls, some of them wonderful Christians, and I know that some of them are pretty and attractive. I want you to be happy like a young man of your age should be, not just a stodgy old lawyer, married to his work. You'll never be as happy as you should be unless you find a good wife and have a family."

"I thought you didn't want the family broken up," he said with a smile.

"You wouldn't be breaking the family up," she retorted. "You would be sure to choose the right kind of girl, one who would become a part of the family. I would be so happy to know that you were happy. Why don't you try to find someone?"

"I suppose, as you say, because I'm already married to my work. And I'm happy in it. Some day, when I sit on the bench like Grandpa, you'll be so proud of me that you won't mind if I'm not married to some beautiful girl."

"You're impossible!" she said. "But I shall keep on praying that God will send you someone who'll sweep you off your feet, or even off that judge's chair and make you happier than you've ever dreamed you could be."

Just then Edwin came in and saw them sitting there.

"What's going on between you two love birds?" he teased.

"A mother hen is trying to persuade her stubborn son that he should find a wife," she told him as she rose and went to him to receive his kiss.

"You see how much better it would be for you to come home to someone waiting to give you a welcome kiss than to just come home to an empty room and open a dull old law book?" Edwin asked.

"I see," Warren said with a smile, "but I'm still satisfied with the law books."

This wasn't quite true, for he wasn't satisfied with those dull law books. He had been thinking of Babs, as he had told his mother, but he had not revealed all his thoughts to her. He was remembering how beautiful she looked the night of her party and how happy she was and how glowing over the present that Bob had sent her, though the gifts were actually Warren's. He was thinking just what his mother had said, of how lonely he would be through the years if he couldn't stop loving this little waif who had become the most precious being in his life. He was hoping that she would find happiness in her love for Bob, though he doubted that Bob could make her happy. Yet he wanted her so much for himself.

Since the night Bob kissed Babs, his attitude toward her had changed. When he saw how pretty she was and realized that she was no longer a little girl, just wanting to tag around after him, sometimes annoyingly, he wanted to take her with him on many of his dates. He was proud of her beauty and since he knew that she still adored him, though with a different adoration than in the years past, it satisfied his vanity to see how pleased she was because he wanted her to go out with him. He didn't stop to think or perhaps he didn't care that she might misunderstand this sudden change in his attitude, that he might lead her to hope that he cared for her. He was thinking only of himself.

There were times when he and his group went on parties together, meeting at some night spot or in the home of one or the other of the girls. As Bob had told Warren, some of these girls belonged to wealthy families and had beautiful homes, and Bob delighted to be invited to them. It gave him a feeling of importance, as if he was really in their class. Though his parents were prosperous, they were far from being wealthy.

He didn't stop to think that none of these young people gave a thought to spiritual matters. God never entered their thoughts. They were absorbed in getting the most fun from life in the way that suited them. Bob followed right along with their thinking. He seemed to have forgotten everything that his mother had taught him. If he didn't forget, he deliberately ignored them.

He was leading Babs along the same path. She was glad to be a part of Bob's social life, to be with him as she used to be when they were in school together. Willing to follow him, no matter where it led her, she didn't even try to remember what she had learned about the Lord. Like Bob and the rest, God was no longer a part of her life. Since she had never surrendered to Him, she drifted with the crowd farther and farther from Him.

There was one thing that kept her from being quite happy

in this new life to which Bob had introduced her. There was a girl, Jessie Hardesty, whose father was immensely wealthy. Jessie entertained the group with parties and dancing and picnics upon the spacious lawn, or with games in the attractive game room when the weather was bad. She was rather pretty and she made no secret of the fact that she preferred Bob above the others.

Babs saw that Bob was flattered and pleased by the girl's attentions and it made her intensely jealous. Jessie seemed to feel her dislike and she was rather cool toward Babs. One evening when they happened to be alone for a few moments, while the others were gathered around the punch bowl, she turned to Babs and remarked, "I never knew that Bob had a sister until recently. I wonder why he never mentioned you before."

"Perhaps he had more interesting things to talk about than a kid sister," Babs replied. "You, for instance."

Jessie didn't return her smile.

"Are you really his sister, or are you just putting one over on us?" she asked. "Funny he never brought you on any of his dates before."

"I've been his sister for a long time, I assure you," Babs told her. "Ask him if he's trying to put one over on you."

"Then why didn't he ever bring you with him before?" Jessie persisted.

"I suppose that Bob just realized lately that I'm no longer just the tomboy sister who always annoyed him by trying to do everything he did and following him everywhere he went. Since he realizes that I'm growing up, I suppose he wants me to begin to have a good time. And I really am having a wonderful time."

"You've surely made a hit with some of the boys," Jessie remarked. "I should be jealous, for one of the boys used to be interested in me, but I'm not. I have Bob and he's the only one I'm interested in."

"You're so pretty that you don't have to be jealous of me," Babs said.

Jessie gave her a hint of a smile as she wandered to where the others were. The boy Jessie mentioned came over to Babs and asked her to come and join the others. She gave him a smile and went with him. *Two can play this little game,* she thought. If Bob was all that Jessie wanted, he was certainly all that Babs wanted, but perhaps if he saw that others thought her attractive, he might be just a little jealous too. She hoped that he would be. The thought that he might care for Jessie frightened her. If that should happen, it would break her heart.

CHAPTER EIGHT

SINCE PEACE HAD BEEN RESTORED in the family, life moved on serenely. The days passed swiftly and weeks slipped into months. They were happy days for Babs. Though Bob had never tried to kiss her again, he did show an interest in her and still took her with him when she didn't have some other boy to take her to the gatherings of their group. She could now think of them as her group also, for she had been accepted as one of them. She accepted the invitation of any boy who asked her for a date. She realized her mistake of past years when she and Bob were in high school together, when she had refused to go with any other boy, for fear that Bob might think she cared for him. Now she wanted him to think that she was interested in other boys.

She was popular with the boys, and some of the girls resented her popularity with them. Even though Bob failed to show any signs of jealousy, he did notice that she was admired by others and it made him more observant of her beauty. He never failed to remark when she looked particularly attractive and this pleased her, though she didn't let him see how pleased she was.

She was contented to let affairs remain as they were, for Bob did not seem particularly interested in Jessie. She hoped that Jessie would lose interest in him.

Whenever she and Bob talked together for long, she emphasized as often as the opportunity presented itself the fact that she was not his real sister. She wanted him to forget that relationship and to think of her as she really was, just a young girl eager for his love.

She mentioned several times how in the past she had been so afraid of Towser and how reluctant Bob had been to accept her.

"What makes you keep bringing that up?" he asked one day. The past now seemed far away. "That's ancient history. I know I was a mean little brat, but I hope I've outgrown some of that meanness. I'll admit that it's a wonder you don't hate me for the way I acted."

"Perhaps so," she replied, "but I adored you so from the very first that I suppose I didn't mind your being mean. You were just yourself and I couldn't hate you. You'll always be my own adored Bobby," she added in tender tones, while her eyes told him more than she realized. "I can't ever forget how all of you took me in when I was so neglected and dirty and I love every one of you for what you've done for me."

"What did I ever do for you, except to boss you and make life miserable for you?" he asked while he observed the look in her eyes and felt uncomfortable because of what he saw there.

"You made a little girl very happy just because you let her play with you. She loved you so much that she didn't mind your bossing. She loved it."

"But you've grown up now and you ought to forget that past. I thought you'd forgotten all about that time Warren found you."

"I did seem to forget it for a long time, but lately it has come back to me. Though I've grown up, my love for that little boy has grown along with me."

"You should really love Warren, for he was the one who found you. If he hadn't been so tenderhearted, you would never have become a part of our family," he told her.

"I know that," and her eyes grew misty at the recollection. "I love him like I would some god, if I worshiped gods. I think I would hate the woman he married, for she might come between us. But the love I have for him isn't the same as what I've always had for that mean little boy who used to tease me and make life miserable, yet happy for me. When you made me cry, I would always run to Warren and find comfort in his arms, but when the tears were dried and I had found the comfort that only he could give, I'd come right back to you to get more of the same treatment. Wasn't I a silly little kid?" she asked with a smile.

"Pretty silly, but I loved it," he admitted. "How would you feel about me if I should marry someone? Would you probably hate her?"

"I'd feel like killing her," she burst out, then, afraid that she had revealed more than she should have, she laughed. "I suppose that dread day will come sometime," she continued, "but I promise that I won't give way to my feelings. I'll pretend to love her while I'll be hating her every minute. But let's talk about something more cheerful than marriages and murders."

"What's more cheerful than marriage?" he wanted to know.

"Don't ask me," and she threw out her hands expressively. "I'm not prepared to answer, since I haven't walked that last mile yet, down to the altar."

"I think that if Jimmie Newton had his way, you'd be walking that mile to meet him any day you named. He's really gone on you, Babs."

"Jimmie's a nice boy and he has been wonderful to me, but I have only friendship to offer him."

"Someday before long some fellow will come along and sweep you off your feet and then I'll be left alone, hating the guy who took you away from me."

"I wish I could believe that you really would feel that way," she said. "I must go and get dressed, or I'll be late for that adoring Jimmie."

She gave his hand a little squeeze, then turned and waved to him as she left him.

He sat there for a while thinking of their conversation. He couldn't fail to see that she loved him. She had practically told him so without actually saying the words. The knowledge had worried him for a time after the talk he had had with Warren before her birthday, but he had ceased to think about it when she became surrounded by other boys and had seemed pleased with their attention. He thought that perhaps she had forgotten "that girlish crush," as Warren had suggested. Now he knew that she hadn't forgotten. He wondered where it would lead them.

She was very beautiful. Other boys desired her, for she was indeed desirable. He remembered the kiss he had given her. He had forgotten that, but now the memory became more vivid as he remembered the touch of her warm lips, the light that leaped into her eyes in that swift moment. Perhaps it would make her happy and he knew that he would enjoy it, if he should make her believe that he cared. It could do no harm, he argued, for she would soon be swept off her feet by someone else. It would be fun while it lasted and if it lasted too long, he could let her down easily, with a quarrel or something. But he wasn't too sure that she wouldn't be hurt, so he put the temptation aside and went to his room to change.

Warren watched Babs' growing maturity and loveliness with longing eyes and a heart that ached with that longing. He was still her counselor and comfort when something seemed to go wrong, for she still came to him with her problems, never dreaming of what he suffered when she gave him some careless caress, leaning on his shoulder or kissing him playfully upon his cheek. The desire to take her in his arms and pour out his love to her was almost more than he could bear.

He worked early and late and he was glad of that, for he didn't come in contact with her very often except at meals. He had engaged in the practice of criminal law, not because he loved the prosecution of criminals, but because he had seen so many sentenced when they were not guilty. His one thought was to help those he could help and to try to make the real criminal see that crime didn't pay.

He had gradually made a reputation for himself and his practice increased more rapidly than he anticipated. Some cases he refused to handle because he knew the person was guilty. He knew that a lawyer could be honest with himself and his fellow man and that a Christian could be a good lawyer and could be above reproach.

The district attorney realized Warren's position and he had grown to respect him, for though he knew that Warren would use everything at his command to defeat a case that he had built up, he knew that Warren would not defend a guilty prisoner. For that reason, when Warren appeared at some trial, the district attorney knew that Warren would use every trick at his command to win his case, for Warren not only had right on his side, but the result of much study and a brilliant mind.

Warren had no desire for publicity, but several of his cases had produced news items and comments upon his skill in handling the case. He felt that the praise was more than he deserved.

He not only studied and worked as a lawyer on a case but as a detective also, and he prayed over every case that he handled.

Warren finally made the headlines in a big way and was started on a career that brought not only fame but heartache into his life.

A young fellow, Frank Sanders, had been arrested and was being held for murder. The evidence was circumstantial, but so convincing that Warren was afraid that the boy would be convicted and executed in spite of all that he might try to do for him. A friend of the prisoner came to Warren, and asked him to take the case. He said he knew the boy was innocent, that he was being railroaded for a crime that someone else had committed. He offered to pay Warren if he would take the case.

When Warren heard the boy's story, he felt that he was innocent. He had been in bad company, but had tried to break away from them. They were afraid that he might talk, for he knew too much, so, after the murder of a night watchman at a warehouse, they left evidence that would tie Frank to the job.

The case was a long-drawn-out affair and the newsmen were there to report every phase of the trial, for there was a battle royal between Warren and the prosecution. It read like some television court scene and the public was avidly interested. The court room was packed each day of the trial. Warren produced all the evidence he could dig up to prove that the boy had been framed, but the prosecution tore down his evidence with witnesses that Warren knew were perjuring themselves. When the case was ended, the prisoner was declared guilty of murder in the first degree and he was sentenced to die.

Warren was not only disappointed at the verdict, but was distressed because he still believed that Frank was innocent and, since the date of the execution had not been set, he determined to use every effort to prove the boy's innocence.

Babs had been present during the trial. She had been intensely interested in the case from the start. She watched the prisoner and wondered how she would feel if she were in his place, with his life hanging in the balance between those two men. She felt sure that the boy wasn't guilty, not only because Warren felt so, but because there was something in the boy's face that made her believe that he was innocent. She knew that this was poor evidence, for sometimes the worst criminals could appear innocent, but she believed him innocent just the same.

Warren's effort to shed new light on the case failed and he began to lose hope of saving the boy. But something happened just before the date set for the execution that gave him hope. One of the gang that Frank had been connected with had been shot as he tried to escape after another killing in a hold-up. He was in the hospital under close guard. Warren went to see the fellow.

At first, when Warren began to talk to him, he was belligerent and refused to talk, though he knew that he was dying. But when Warren continued to talk to him, not as a lawyer, but as a Christian, trying to witness to him of the love of Christ who gave His life as a ransom for all, the fellow began to listen and his venom and belligerence vanished.

He told Warren that he had never heard anything like what Warren had been telling him, but when Warren paused for a moment, the fellow's eyes became hard again and he said, "You're just trying to soften me up so I'll confess that I killed the man Frank's gonna hang for. He deserves hanging for walking out on us. Let him hang. I won't be here to see it, but he'll get what's comin' to him."

"Have you thought of what's coming to you, fellow, if you go out into eternity a lost soul?" Warren asked. "I'm not only trying to get you to confess that Frank is innocent, but I'm trying to get you to see that unless you repent of your sins and get forgiveness in the little time you have left, you'll join Frank in an endless place of torment."

"I don't believe in hell," the fellow cried while he winced with pain. "It's something cooked up by preachers to scare people into coming to church. They're just after money and the saps don't know no better than to believe that hogwash."

"I'm afraid that you'll learn to your sorrow that it isn't hogwash," Warren said seriously. "It's true, every word that I've told you. Christ died on the cross to save sinners like you and sinners like me from the hell that was prepared for the devil and his angels. His only requisite is that we come to Him and ask for the gift of eternal life, so that we will be with Him throughout eternity and not in that place of torment. That gift was given to the thief on the cross beside Him. That same gift is offered to you now, if you'll receive it."

He shook his head. "It's too late now. I can't believe. I don't think God would hear me. I've gone too far."

"But you can save Frank's life and give him a chance, so that perhaps one day he may believe. Won't you give him that chance?" Warren asked. "He's so young that he can't be all bad. When he walked out on your gang, he was trying to start a clean life. Why not give him a chance? Why carry his blood on your hands? Don't you think you have enough to answer for without that?"

There were tears in the hardened eyes of the dying man as he nodded.

"You're right," he muttered. "No use having Frank's blood on my hands. They're already carrying too much," and he held them up for a moment. "I killed that night watchman. Frank never killed anyone. He was too good for our gang. He got in before he knew just what we were."

Warren turned to the officer on guard.

"Will you be willing to witness to what you've just heard?" he asked.

"Sure I will," the officer answered.

He had listened with interest to what Warren had said and Warren could see that the man had been impressed. He hoped that the seed sowed might one day bear fruit in this man's life.

He hastily wrote the fellow's confession and then asked him to sign it. The weak hand scrawled his name across the page, then the officer added his name. Warren called in the nurse and asked her to read what he had written and then asked the prisoner to verify his confession. He nodded and said that it was true. Then the nurse signed her name.

The newspapers carried headlines saying that the verdict against Frank Sanders had been reversed. The case had been reopened and the evidence that Warren had brought proved the boy's innocence. The leading paper carried an editorial which praised Warren to the highest. The officer on guard had told what he had witnessed and heard and the paper commented upon the unusual approach to the dying prisoner.

Warren was sorry about that part of the editorial. He didn't want the public to think that he had merely used his witnessing as a trick to get a prisoner to confess. Those who didn't understand would think it was just that and nothing more. They wouldn't know that he was just as much interested in the soul of a dying criminal as he was concerned with saving the life of Frank Sanders.

The news item and the editorial put Warren in the public eye and led him one step nearer the goal which he had hoped to reach in the years when it was just a young boy's dream.

CHAPTER NINE

As WARREN WATCHED BABS and saw how her eyes glowed and observed her happy smile, he knew the reason for her joy. Bob admired her and wanted her to be with him and to share his outings with his group. She was happy to be near him and to be a part of his life again, even though that life was leading them both in the wrong direction.

He tried not to be jealous of Bob, but sometimes it rose within him in spite of his effort to control it. Bob was taking for granted with indifference something that Warren felt that he would give anything in the world to possess. He saw how Babs' face lighted up when she came in looking especially lovely and heard Bob's comment about how attractive she looked. She accepted his own remarks as a matter of course and though she gave him a smile and a word of thanks for some compliment, or else gave him a careless caress, he knew that what he said meant little to her. It was what she expected from him, but Bob's compliment was the thing she was looking for and eager to receive.

His heart ached when he saw them going out to some party, for he knew what kind of an evening they would be having. He knew the way they were living was breaking his mother's heart, but there was nothing he could do about it. As his father had said, they couldn't be coerced into something that they rebelled against. Unless the Holy Spirit brought them under conviction, there was nothing they could do but pray.

"I believe she'd follow that boy to hell," Edwin remarked one day wrathfully after he had had another talk with Bob and had gotten nowhere.

"That's just what she is doing," Mary replied sadly. "If they only realized that they are on their way there and that they don't know when they may be called upon to give an account of their lives, perhaps they might yield to God, but they just won't listen. And after all my teaching when they were little children. It makes me almost wonder about that verse in Proverbs, 'Train up a child in the way he should go and when he is old he will not depart from it.' I tried to train them up in the way they should go, but they surely aren't following my teachings."

"They didn't do the one thing necessary," Edwin said. "They refused to accept the Lord and receive the gift of eternal life and salvation from Him."

"I tried to get them to accept the Lord, but some perverse spirit made them refuse to do that. With Warren it was so easy. He accepted the Lord the first time I put the question to him and he's never gotten away from the Lord. I'm thankful that I have one son at least whom I can be proud of. I'm surely not proud of Bob or Babs."

"We can't give up hope that one day God will answer our prayers," he said as he put an arm around her and kissed her tenderly.

Even though Warren had given up hope of winning Babs, he didn't grow morose or bitter. He plunged deeper into his work and put all of himself into it. His reputation grew, though he wasn't trying for publicity.

During the year he was successful in defending several cases that drew wide attention and his name appeared more frequently in the local papers. He drew the attention of certain members of one of the two political parties in the city and they made their plans to use him on their ticket during the next election. They said nothing to him, but they had several secret caucuses and discussed the situation. They wanted him for judge of the first city criminal court. The present incumbent was getting quite old and they feared that if he were re-elected, he would not last the term out. They wanted control of that office and they decided to make their plans before they approached Warren.

Babs still came to Warren with her problems as she had always done and sometimes these little interviews strained him terribly. He found it difficult to keep his role of big brother adviser and not to yield to the impulse to take her in his arms and pour out his love to her.

Sometimes, in his effort to restrain himself, he became more remote than usual and then she would look at him gravely and say, "Warren, dear, am I boring you?"

"No! No!" he would exclaim. "You never could do that. I was just weighing your problem. I want you to do the right thing about that boy who is so persistent. You know that."

"Of course I do," she told him. "You're such a darling," and she gave him a careless kiss upon his cheek. "What would I do without you? What would I do if some designing female should come along and take you from me? How I would hate her!"

"You wouldn't want me to be lonely all my life, would you?" he asked gravely.

"Are you lonely?" she asked in surprise.

"Sometimes, very, very lonely," he said with a note of sadness in his voice.

"I never thought of you as being lonely," she admitted thoughtfully. "You have Mom and Dad — and me," she added playfully. "How could you be lonely?"

"But I don't have you," he told her. "Bob has all there is of you."

"Yes, he has all there is of my heart, except for one very special place that I've reserved for you. You shall always have that place, as long as I live. I love you so much, Warren dear, more than anyone in the world besides Bob. But then, I've told you that so many times that it's an old story and I know it bores you."

"It doesn't bore me. It makes me very happy," he told her while he struggled to keep from taking her in his arms and kissing her with no big brotherly kiss. "But have you ever thought that perhaps I'd want someone who gave me all of her heart, just as you've given Bob all of yours? That without that kind of love from someone, my life will never be completely happy?"

"I never thought of it in that way," she admitted. "I've just been thinking of myself, how happy I am to have you and to love you so much. I would hate to see you love someone as much as I love Bob, for then you wouldn't have any time for me and I'd feel left out of your life entirely. It just wouldn't seem fair. That is selfish, isn't it?" and she gave him a faint smile. The thought was worrying her.

"Is there someone that you love in the way that I love Bob?" she asked with a worried frown.

"There is, but that is a secret that I may never be able to tell you," he replied with a slow smile. "Let's get back to this fellow who's been so persistent and forget about us. You're happy with Bob and I shall try to keep you happy, so be happy."

"But I'm not happy with Bob," she denied. "I don't think he cares a thrip about me in the way I care for him and I'd give my right arm for just a little of his love. I've almost given up hope that he'll ever care."

"Don't give up, just keep on being beautiful and perhaps one day he'll see what a priceless prize he has in you. If you belonged to the Lord and if you let Him take control of your life, you would be able to pray about Bob and believe that if it was the Lord's will, he would love you as you love him, but since you are not the Lord's, you don't even have the privilege of asking Him anything."

"Now don't start preaching," she cried. "I get enough of that from Mom. I want Bob, whether it's 'the Lord's will' or not, and if I can't have his love, I just don't care what becomes of me."

"That's a pretty reckless and dangerous thing to say, little one," he cautioned. "I shall pray that one day you will be able to say to the Lord, 'Thy will be done,' and in the meantime I shall pray for you that His will may be done between you and Bob. I know that whatever His will is, it will be for your good. My one wish for you is that you may be happy and happy in the Lord and not in your own careless way of life."

He sat there for a long time after she had left, wondering what the future would hold for them all, for Babs and Bob in their selfish and sinful way of life. He thought of himself in his loneliness and heartache, of his future and what it would be without her.

When he prayed that night, he prayed for Babs, that she would find happiness in Bob's love, if that were His will, but that, above all and in spite of what might come to her, that she would come to know Christ as her Saviour and realize that this was the only life that would bring real happiness and peace.

CHAPTER TEN

WARREN WON ANOTHER SENSATIONAL VICTORY that brought him into the limelight again. A man by the name of Jim Anderson had been arrested as an accomplice in a murder connected with a car theft. Jim was identified by someone who had witnessed the killing as one of the three who fled from the crime.

Warren believed that the prisoner was innocent, in spite of the evidence against him, and he fought the case with every art he possessed. While the trial was in progress, one of the bandits was brought in. He had been arrested as he was trying to steal another car. His likeness to Jim Anderson was so striking that it amazed the court. He was put on the stand and Warren finally forced a confession from him that he was the one who had committed the murder and not Jim, that Jim was not a member of the gang.

Babs was at the trial as usual. She was there every time she could attend when Warren was on a case. She marveled at the way he threw his questions at a witness for the prosecution. He was never rough or angry in his questioning, but he fired the questions with such rapidity that often the witness was unable to think clearly and was confused in his answers. When this trial was ended and Warren's client was exonerated, Babs could hardly wait for the court to clear so she could go to Warren and congratulate him.

Though many crowded around him and congratulated him, prominent men in the legal profession, Warren was as eager as a youngster to hear what Babs had to say. He saw her standing at the edge of the crowd and as they melted away, he motioned her to come to him.

"I'm so proud of you!" she exclaimed. "I just sat there and

hung upon your every word and how it thrills me to see you win a victory over that self-confident district attorney. It's such a privilege that I can claim you as my big brother."

He smiled at her and thanked her for her interest in his work.

"It means more to me than you can imagine," he told her.

"Why shouldn't I be interested in whatever you do?" she asked. "You're a part of my life. The best part of it," she added.

When they reached his office, she plopped down upon his his knee, something she hadn't done since she was a little girl and it surprised him. She looked very grave and he wondered what was troubling her.

"What's on your mind, little one?" he asked.

She put her arm around his neck and leaned against his shoulder.

"I've been thinking," she said in slow, serious voice. "I sat there thinking during that whole trial, of what you had done for me since that day when you found me. If it hadn't been for you and what your love and kindness has meant to me all through the years, I might have been what so many other young people are. I might be standing before the bar of justice like some of those others, instead of having a wonderful happy home life, an adored mother and father and a big brother like you. If I should live a hundred years, I can never cease thanking you for what you did for me that day you found me."

"Why Babs, you surprise me," he exclaimed. "I was hoping that you had forgotten about that. You were so little and you scarcely ever mentioned it. What brought that up?"

"I did seem to forget it for years. As you say, I was so little and I was so happy to be rid of that awful life when I was so alone and so often hungry and neglected. I'm sure I must have been or I wouldn't have been lost that day you found me. I accepted my new life and was happy in it, but lately I seem to remember dimly things that I never could remember before, little things that seem like a dream, but things that sometimes worry me.

"I remember so vividly that day you brought me to your home, but I can't remember my mother. I don't remember what she looked like. All I remember is that I didn't love her and that when your mother told me that I was to stay with her and be her little girl, I was so happy that I forgot even to think of my mother again. What happened to her, Warren? Mom told me that she went away and that she wouldn't be coming back and I accepted that, but lately I have wondered just what did happen to her. Did she run away and leave me to starve?"

"No, dear, she didn't do that. I'm sure that she must have loved you. She died very suddenly."

"How did she die?" Babs persisted.

"All that I can tell you is that she died of natural causes. Now let's talk of something more cheerful. How about going with me to lunch? Or do you have a date with the very special member of the family?" He gave her a playful smile.

"No, that very special member of the family is too much occupied with his new position in Dad's firm. He feels his importance so that sometimes I feel that he's forgotten my existence. I'd love to go to lunch with you. In a way, you're more special than he is," she added as she gave him a peck upon his cheek.

He put an arm around her and held her a moment while he struggled against the desire to kiss her.

Babs felt like a celebrity herself as they entered the restaurant. There were many people who knew Warren and others who knew who he was. Many eyes were turned upon them as they went to their table.

"I feel as if I was in the shadow of royalty," she remarked as they sat down. "You're the center of attraction and I'm just reveling in the reflected light of your glory."

"I think most of those who stare at us are looking at the very beautiful young lady who is with me," he told her.

"Perhaps they're wondering if I'm THE ONE, that mysterious person whose name is such a secret," she said with a mischievous twinkle in her eyes.

"Perhaps they'd be disappointed to know that there was no romance for them to speculate about, that you're just a very lovely sister. But those two young friends of mine over there might be even more interested to know that, as yet, there are no strings that bind you to anyone."

She looked at him and he saw something in her eyes that he had never seen there before, and she said slowly as she gave him that look, half adoring, half just admiration, "It would be such an honor to be your wife. I know that mysterious person must feel that way. If I were your wife, I'd be as proud as if I were the first lady of the land."

Her words took him so by surprise that for a moment he stared at her, speechless while he fought against the words that wanted to burst forth. He fought the desire to tell her that if she only would, she could be his wife and that she would make him happier than if he were a king of the greatest kingdom on earth.

Instead he finally managed to say, "What on earth brought that up?"

"I was thinking of that mysterious person whose name is such a secret. I almost envy her, for she will be so safe and secure with you. You would make any woman happy, for you're so thoughtful and so gentle and kind. You're so wonderful! But there I go saying the same thing over again."

"My! My!" he exclaimed. "What can I say in answer to all that flattery? Are you forgetting Bob while you're throwing all those bouquets at me?"

"I'm not forgetting him at all," she replied seriously, "but even if he should fall in love with me, he could never make me as happy as you will make some woman. I adore him and if I never have his love, I shall want to die, but I still envy that woman you will one day marry. Is that what you call being all mixed up or just plain silly?"

He smiled and said with a tender note in his voice. "It's neither, my dear. You're in love with the rascal who will one day appreciate you for what you are and today you're in a hero-worshiping mood. Not that I'm a hero by any means," he added. "What you have said makes me happier than you will ever know. When I get to be an old man and have been set aside by the world, I shall still remember what you have said today and when I think of those words, my heart will skip a beat and I'll feel that I'm having a heart attack."

She laughed. "Now it's you who is being silly. I don't know how all this got started, but I do know that I'm hungry. Shall we order?"

They both laughed, for the waiter had long since left them to their own little world while he took another order elsewhere.

Among those who came to the table to congratulate Warren were the two young men he had mentioned. When they spoke to him, they looked hopefully at Babs. He introduced her as his sister and their interest was directed toward her. They lingered longer than was necessary, talking to her.

"You've made a double conquest," Warren told her when they had left. "I told you that would happen."

When they parted and Warren returned to his office, he was not in the frame of mind to finish any business. He was thinking of what Babs had said. She would be proud to be his wife. It would be such an honor to be his wife. He clenched his fists for a moment and then bowed his head on his arms upon his desk while he fought against unmanly tears. After a time he raised his head and plunged into his work, but the zeal and joy of it had vanished.

While Babs was on her way home, she too was remembering their conversation. She had forgotten about her real mother, for she had never been too concerned about her. She was a shadow out of the past, a shadow connected with unhappy memories that flitted through her mind like some bad dream and which she refused to harbor for long. Why had she said what she had to Warren? It was true, even though she loved Bob with all her heart. She would be proud to be Warren's wife. It would be an honor and she knew that he would make her happy, that he would make any woman happy. She would want to be his wife if it wasn't for Bob. But Bob was the center of her life, the hope of every heart beat. Without his love, life would be a "dead oyster," as Bob sometimes expressed it when things went wrong. Her heart would be dead within her and life would have no meaning.

CHAPTER ELEVEN

WARREN WAS SADDENED ONE MORNING to read of the sudden death of Judge Hanson, judge of the first criminal court. He had known the judge for many years. The judge had helped Warren when he was studying law and had encouraged him in his ambition. Warren wondered who would replace him until the next election.

The judge's death shocked those in the inner political circle. They had made their plans to put Warren up for election in the coming race, but now they must make a decision about a replacement immediately. They finally decided to go to Warren. They told him what their plans had been and urged him to let them name him for appointment to fill the vacancy until the election.

This came as a complete surprise to Warren and he asked them to give him time to think it over. They told him that they must know at once, for a successor had to be named in the shortest possible time. There were important cases on the docket and the other judge couldn't handle them all. They were sure that if Warren would consent, he would be appointed. Their party was in power in the city and they knew that they could control the appointee.

Warren told them that he would let them know the next day. It was the culmination of his ambition, a dream he had had ever since he was old enough to know what it meant, but now that it had come, he wondered whether he should accept the appointment or not. He was still young for the position and he had had so little experience in the short time he had been practicing that he wondered if he was ready for that important office.

It was an honor for them to want him when he was so young. He appreciated the honor and he couldn't help but feel thrilled about it. He was also humbly grateful. He knew that if he made good, he would be the logical candidate for election. He had thought that if he ever had the courage to run for that office, he would have to fight his way to the top, but now it was practically handed to him without any effort on his part to reach his goal.

He finally decided to accept and he told the committee so when they came for his answer. They were jubilant, since they now saw victory for them in the coming election, for, if Warren made good, he would be practically without opposition.

A few days later the papers carried Warren's picture on the front page with quite a write-up. It gave a brief account of his life, mentioning the fact that his grandfather had once sat on this same bench and that Warren was the youngest criminal judge who had ever served.

Babs was much excited over the appointment. She cut out the article and the picture and pasted it in her book of memories.

"I shall keep it as an heirloom for my grandchildren," she told him. "This isn't the only thing about you that I have in my book of memories," she said. "I have all the little articles that appeared in your high school paper about you and the picture of you when you graduated from high school and also when you got your degree from law school. It's your book of memories as well as mine."

"It must be a tremendous treasure," he said laughingly.

"You have no idea what a treasure it is," she told him seriously. "Even if you marry that secret love of yours, I'll still have a part of you with me always. She can't take that away from me."

"How about Bob?" he asked. "Do you have a book of memory of him?"

She shrugged and shook her head.

"There never was anything to put. He never did anything that was worth mentioning at school except a few escapades that he was glad to have forgotten. But I won't need a book of memory for him," she added with a serious, wistful look in her expressive eyes. "I have him in my heart and I'll remember every little word that he ever said to me that gave me hope that he would love me. They will remain in my heart if I live to be a thousand, even if I never have him."

"I envy Bob," he said, bursting out without thinking.

"Why?" she asked in surprise. "You have everything that you have ever wanted in life. Why should you envy anyone, least of all Bob?"

"It's too complicated to explain, so let's forget it," he said, sorry that the words had slipped out. "Do you have a date for tomorrow night?"

"No," she said. "The gang was to go on a moonlight picnic, but the ground is too wet, so they called it off. I'm glad they did, for Tommy Fairley would have been my date and he bores me to tears. He won't let me alone. When he's around, I can't even get a word in edgewise with Bob. Bob will think I care for him and I don't want that."

"That's the very thing you should want," Warren advised her. "If Bob sees that such a good looking fellow as Tommy has attracted you, it might arouse his interest. It might help him to see what he is losing."

"I tried that before, but it didn't work, but, as you say, it's worth trying again. But what do you have in mind for tomorrow night?"

"Some of my political friends are giving me a dinner at the Henderson Hotel, a sort of testimonial dinner they call it, but I think it's a little previous. Mom and Dad will be there and I want you to go as my guest."

"How wonderful!" she exclaimed. "I shall feel more like a queen than I did when you took me to dinner after that trial. This time I will surely shine in reflected glory. Isn't Bob going?" she asked.

"He said he had a date and couldn't come," Warren told her.

"A date!" she echoed. "I wonder who it's with."

All her exuberance left her. He felt sorry for her and was sorry that he had told her about Bob, but he knew that she would find out soon enough.

"Couldn't Bob have broken the date for such an important event?" she asked.

"Perhaps he didn't think my date was important enough. I thought he might break his date, but since he didn't seem interested enough to do so, I wouldn't ask him to. He's a pretty self-centered fellow, you know, and is only interested in the things that contribute to his own happiness or desires. I hope that some day he will outgrow that and that the best that is in him will come to the surface. He has possibilities."

The dinner was a success both from a social standpoint and as a tribute to Warren and his prowess. Babs was thrilled at the testimonials that were given in the brief after-dinner speeches and the many well wishers who came to him after the dinner and congratulated him. She met most of the prominent men in the city's affairs and she was thrilled at that, but underneath all the thrill of being with him and being, as she said, in reflected glory, was the thought of Bob's indifference. He never seemed interested in anyone or anything that didn't fit in with his own little plans for his life. She wished that he might be more like Warren and she felt hurt to know that he had a date with some girl after their party had fallen through.

Warren's first case as judge proved a difficult one. There had been so many cases on the docket when the judge died suddenly that Warren was kept busy from the beginning. Some of the cases were minor offenses and were soon decided, but others were more serious. One of them was regarding a member of a narcotics gang that had been operating for some months in the city. He had been arrested while passing a package of heroin.

The case created a lot of interest in the local papers. The lawyer for the defense fought to get his client off with a light sentence or an acquittal. Warren knew that he was being paid by the ring that had hired him. The evidence against the prisoner was too convincing and all the efforts of the defense failed. The police had been on the case for quite a while, for they were anxious to get the head of the gang.

Warren gave the prisoner the maximum sentence. As he was being taken from the court room, the man turned and shook his fist at Warren and shouted, "I'll get you for this, you just wait and see what happens to you!"

Babs, as usual, was at the trial, and she was frightened

by the prisoner's shouted vengeance. She was nervous and anxious and as soon as Warren came home, she spoke to him about it.

"Aren't you afraid of what that fellow will do to you?" she asked. "He looked like he could have murdered you right there."

"Not much chance of him carrying out his threat any time soon. By the time he gets out of prison, he will have had time to change his mind about vengeance," Warren told her. "However, that's one thing a judge has to expect. More than one judge has been killed by some prisoner seeking vengeance. One thing sure — I won't die or be killed until the Lord is finished with me here. When that day comes, I won't be afraid to go, for I know that I'm ready. But you don't have that assurance, Babs, because you're not ready to go when God says, 'It's enough.' Have you never thought of that?"

"I don't want to think about it," she said, "so please don't start preaching. I'm not afraid for myself, but for you. No one has threatened my life."

"But I'm not afraid for myself, dear, but for you. Eternity may stretch before you sooner than it may for me and I know you're not prepared to face it."

She turned away but he caught her and held her for a moment while he looked searchingly into her eyes.

"Don't be angry, honey," he said gently. "You can never understand how anxious I am about your soul. I'd give my life this very minute to have you accept Christ as your Saviour and to know that your soul is safe in His hands."

"Do you really mean that?" she asked.

"I really mean it."

"Why do you?"

"Because I love you enough to want to see you safe through all eternity and not walking upon a dangerous path that can only lead to one end, regret and eternal suffering."

He bent and kissed her gently upon her forehead and then released her.

She was stirred by what he had said and by the look in his eyes as he held her. Why did she feel that warmth within her every time she saw this little spark in his eyes or the tender note in his voice? She was not thinking about what he had said concerning her soul, she was thinking how this had stirred something within her that puzzled and confused her. She wished she knew who Warren was in love with, she thought illogically. If she didn't love him, what a sap she must be.

CHAPTER TWELVE

BABS DECIDED TO ACT UPON WARREN'S SUGGESTION and accept the boring attentions of Tommy Fairley. He was good looking and had money besides, but that didn't make Babs the least bit interested in him. She wanted Bob and no one else. But as Warren had suggested, if Bob saw that a boy like Tommy was interested in her and that she seemed interested in him, it might arouse the love she longed for.

As she had told Warren, she had tried it before, but this was when Bob had been deeply engrossed with Jessie Hardesty. She noticed lately that they had not seemed so friendly and she hoped that now Bob might show some signs of jealousy.

Tommy hovered over her as if she already belonged to him and this irritated her, but she bore it with a smile and pretended to be pleased with his attentions. To her great joy, Bob began to notice and to speculate about this new turn of events. Until now Babs had showed so plainly that she wasn't interested in anyone but himself that he took her devotion for granted. It flattered and pleased him and he expected it to continue. He didn't know how it might end but he was not concerned about that.

Now he thought that she must really be interested in Tommy and it irked him to think that she no longer cast longing eyes at him when she saw him with some other girl or was herself hemmed in by some other boy. She never gave him a glance and when their eyes met, she gave him a cool glance and then turned her attention to someone else.

Jealousy rose within him. She was very beautiful and he felt that she belonged to him in a very special way, but now there was someone else claiming her and she seemed willing to forget the adoration she had had for him. Now that she seemed about to slip away from him, he wanted her love. He had always accepted it with indifference, feeling that it would never change. He didn't want someone else to take what was his.

"You seem mighty interested in Tommy Fairley," he remarked when they had come home one evening.

Tommy had scarcely left her for a moment. She had no opportunity even to talk to another boy. The other boys began to tease Tommy about Babs, but Tommy enjoyed their teasing.

"I'd marry her tomorrow if she'd have me," he told them.

"Why shouldn't I be interested in Tommy?" Babs asked Bob. "He's good looking and he does everything he can to make me have a good time. I'd be mighty ungrateful if I didn't show my appreciation."

"Is that all you feel for him?" he asked with a relieved note in his voice.

"I didn't say that," she countered. "I like him a lot."

She saw that he was jealous and she thrilled at the knowledge.

"He never gives anyone else a chance to get in a word with you," he grumbled. "It doesn't seem right for you to tie yourself down to one boy. That's not the way to be popular. You should treat them all alike."

"Even if I cared more for one than all the others?" she asked.

He caught her by the shoulders and held her while he looked at her grimly.

"Are you in love with that fellow?" he demanded.

"What if I am?" she asked with a provocative smile. "What difference would that make to you?"

"A lot," he admitted. "I feel that you belong to me and I don't want some other fellow to come along and take you away from me."

"I belong to you!" she cried with pretended surprise. "Whatever gave you that idea?"

"Didn't you always care for me more than you did for anyone else? That's what you've always said."

"Oh that," she scoffed. "That was when I was a little kid

and didn't know any better. Now that I'm older, I see things in a different light. You have other girls who claim your attention and perhaps you're in love with one of them, Jessie, for instance, so why shouldn't I outgrow that childish adoration and find someone I can love as a girl should love?"

"You mean that you don't care for me any longer?" he asked in grieved tones.

"Oh, I care for my big brother as I always shall," she said, trying to appear far from what she was feeling, "but childish adoration and grown-up love are two different feelings entirely."

"I don't want you to love anyone but me," he said and he tried to draw her to him.

She wanted to be held in his arms, but she pulled away from him.

"Do you want to be a dog in the manger?" she asked. "You don't love me as a girl should be loved, but you don't want me to love anyone else. What do you want me to do, become an old maid, worshiping you while some other girl has your love and eventually has you? How selfish can you get?"

He drew her to him, in spite of her effort to resist him and held her close.

"I am selfish," he admitted. "I've always taken you for granted because I was so sure that you loved me. Now I'm afraid that you're slipping away from me. I want you, Babs dear. I would be lost without you and your love. I can't live without it, honey. I love you, Babs. I really do love you. Don't let me down. I want your love. I want you. Forget that Tommy fellow. Just say you haven't stopped loving me. Say that you still do."

"I wonder if you really love me, Bob, or if you're just trying to keep me hanging around as I've always done, while you give your love to someone else."

"I love you, Babs darling," he insisted. "I've always thought of you as belonging to me. I want you to belong to me always. I love you! I love you! Tell me that you haven't outgrown the love you had for me."

She leaned against his breast and a sigh escaped her, a sigh of utter joy. The unbelievable had happened. She had won! Bob really loved her. It seemed impossible and she could scarcely believe it.

"What's your answer, Babs darling?" he asked as she remained silent.

"You should know the answer," she said as she lifted her face and looked into his eyes. "You should know that I couldn't ever love anyone but you. I've loved you ever since that first day you let me play with Towser. I love you so much, Bob, so very much! I'd want to die if you ever let me down."

He bent and kissed her while she clung to him and joy flowed through her. He held her for a moment, then kissed her again and let her go, for he heard Warren's car coming into the driveway.

"I'll never let you down," he whispered as he left her and went to his room.

She waited for Warren. She had to tell him the wonderful news. He found her sitting starry-eyed upon the divan.

"Something wonderful happen?" he asked, for the signs were unmistakable.

"Something very wonderful," she said. "Sit down for a minute and let me tell you about it."

He sat beside her and took one of her hands.

"Let's have it," he said.

"Bob just told me that he loved me. Oh, Warren, it's so wonderful! I can scarcely believe it. Your suggestion about Tommy worked. He said he was afraid he would lose me when he saw me so interested in Tommy." She laughed happily. "If he just knew how I suffered with that bore hanging around me all the time. But I have him to thank for bringing Bob to his senses. I'm so happy that I just can't believe it," she sighed. "Wish me happiness, big brother."

"I do," he said with a smile. "Your happiness means more to me than you can ever know. But I think I've said that before. I hope and pray that Bob will make you the happiest girl in the world."

They arose and Babs put her arms around his neck and gave him a kiss upon his cheek.

"You'll always let me come to you with my troubles, won't you?" she asked anxiously. "Because Bob loves me doesn't mean that I love you any the less. I shall always love you and want to come to you for comfort, so don't ever fail me, please."

"I just hope that you won't ever need to come to me for comfort when you and Bob are happy together," he said tenderly. "I hope that he'll make you so happy that you won't need me any more."

"I'll always need you," she insisted. "If it was you instead of Bob, I would be sure that I'd never need anyone but you, but with Bob I'm not so sure. But no matter what happens to me or to our love, I'll always keep you in my heart and love you best of all, next to him."

He watched her as she closed the door of her room behind her. He sat down for a moment longer, thinking of what she had said. So it had happened, the thing he wished for her, yet the thing that he dreaded to see happen. He tried to be happy for her, but he couldn't control the pain in his heart.

As he prayed, he tried to pray that Babs would be happy in the love of Bob, but he found it difficult to pray sincerely, for the longing for her was greater than his desire for her happiness, when that happiness was with someone else.

CHAPTER THIRTEEN

Bob met Babs the next morning as she was leaving her room. She gave him a smile while her eyes lighted with the joy that bubbled forth from her.

"Good morning, Bob darling," she said.

He caught her to him and kissed her swiftly, for he knew that she was waiting for it.

"Let's not tell anyone about us yet," he said as he held her. "If we do, Mom and Dad will start planning our future and that's something we want to do for ourselves. And our crowd won't understand if they know. They think you're my real sister and it might cause complications. Let's wait a while until we know just what we want to do."

"But I've already told Warren," she admitted. "I was so happy that I had to tell him. I think he would have guessed if I hadn't. I waited up to tell him last night."

"I'm sorry you did that," Bob said with a worried frown. "He'll start preaching to me right away about how I should act and what we should do. You warn him not to tell anyone for a while, that we want to make our own plans. I know he'll understand and he'll keep off my neck. At least I hope he does."

"I'll do whatever you say," she agreed, though she was disappointed. She was so happy that she wanted to tell the news to the whole world. "If you don't want anyone to know about us, then I suppose you want me to continue to let Tommy think that he's tops with me."

"No, I don't want that," he stated emphatically. "I don't want that fellow hanging around you. Can't you give him the gate? Let him know that you're tired of him hanging around, that he's taking up too much of your time. Tell him that you want to be popular with everyone and not just tied down with him. You can do it in a nice way, so that he won't be offended. I'm sure you can."

"Does that apply to you and Jessie?" she asked. "Are you going to give her the gate?"

"I can't do that," he said lamely. "She's done a lot for me. She's introduced me to a lot of influential people and she got me into her crowd. I never would have been accepted if it hadn't been for her. Her father likes me and he may make me an offer to work in his firm."

"What's the matter with Dad's firm?" she asked in surprise. "I thought you were so happy when he took you in."

"I was, but there's not nearly the opportunity in Dad's business that there is in Mr. Hardesty's. There would be more opportunity for me there, because his firm is so much bigger than Dad's."

"Do you think he would still be interested in you if he knew that you were in love with me and not with Jessie?" she asked as a little doubt crept in.

"What has Jessie got to do with it?" he asked rather crossly.

"A lot, I'm afraid. I know that she's in love with you. If you turn her down for me, I wonder if it wouldn't change his idea about taking you into his firm?"

Her eyes gazed unsmilingly into his.

"You're jealous of Jessie," he said. "That's what's worrying you."

"Yes, I'm jealous of her," she admitted. "I'm jealous of anyone who has her eyes on you possessively. I've always been jealous of anyone like her. You'll never be able to know how much I love you, Bob," she said while she gave him an adoring look. "I've always thought that you belonged to me and I hated anyone who looked as if they were trying to take you away from me. I hate Jessie and I begrudge every minute you spend with her. If you really love me, as you said you did, you wouldn't want her any more than I want Tommy."

"I don't," he maintained stoutly, "but the circumstances are different. My future may depend upon Mr. Hardesty's offer and I want the best for both of us. Isn't that what you want too?"

"Not if it makes you continue to pretend something for Jessie that you don't really feel," she said.

"Stop worrying about her," he said. "I'm not going to pretend anything for her that I don't feel. I love you and so you can be satisfied. Everything will work out, I'm sure, so stop worrying and let's be happy together because we love each other."

She had to be satisfied with this, though there was still a little doubt in her heart. She was still afraid that Jessie's wealth and Mr. Hardesty's interest in Bob might win him away from her. She had to be content with things as they were, so she decided to try not to worry about something that she couldn't control.

Mary noticed that Babs was very happy about something, but she didn't ask what it was. She knew that if Babs wanted her to know, she would tell her.

When breakfast was over and Warren had a few minutes alone with Bob, he told Bob what Babs had told him.

"I'm glad for you both," he said. "All her life she has adored you and I think it would have broken her heart if you hadn't fallen in love with her. I do hope that you two will be happy together."

"Thanks," Bob replied. "We've decided not to tell anyone for a while. We want to wait until we've decided what to do for the future, before we even tell Dad and Mom. You know how they will be. They'll try to make plans for us and we don't want that."

"The only thing that Mom will be concerned about is that both of you may accept the Lord before you start out life together," Warren said. "She knows that two young people beginning life together need the Lord more than ever. That will be her prayer for you, Bob, so don't forget that. Take time to think of it. You know as well as I do that salvation is the most important thing in life, for it decides where you will spend eternity. With it you have everything. Without it you have nothing, no matter how much of this world's wealth you might accumulate."

Bob held up his hand and exclaimed, "That's enough, Judge. Save your sermons for the ones who stand before you, for they surely need them more than I do."

"I doubt that," Warren replied.

"Well, I'm not in the mood to listen. I've got more important things on my mind. Thanks again, big brother, for your good wishes."

He left Warren with a wave of his hand and a quick exit.

Warren looked after him and there was a grave expression upon his face. What would the end be, he wondered. Would Bob ever yield to the call of the Spirit? He knew that every time Bob was faced with the call to accept the Lord and he refused, a hardening process took place. That was inevitable. Would he wait until he was so hardened that he would never yield? If that should happen, Warren knew it would break his mother's heart, for her heart was already burdened with Bob's indifference.

Babs and Bob continued practically as they had been. When they went out to join the group at some affair, they usually went together. Bob always drifted to Jessie's side. She managed that and Babs was miserable with jealousy as she saw Jessie's possessive air, as if Bob belonged to her.

She decided that she would tolerate Tommy and that she wouldn't do as Bob had suggested, so he still remained her faithful shadow. She didn't think that Bob played fair with her for wanting her to break off with Tommy while he still continued to pay so much attention to Jessie.

She told him as much one evening when Tommy had been with her most of the time and when Bob complained about it as they were on their way home.

"If you'll play fair with me, I'll play fair with you," she told him. "As long as you continue to pay so much attention to Jessie and let her think she owns you, I'll continue to let Tommy think that he's the only one for me. I don't think this can go on much longer. Either you let us tell all of them the truth, or let me believe that you don't really love me."

"I'll tell Jessie the truth very soon," he promised. "For the present, please be patient. Her father has already made me that offer. While I'm thinking it over, let's let things remain as they are."

"While you continue to let Jessie think that you love her," she accused. "That's not honest and I don't like it, Bob."

"Have patience and everything will work out all right," he promised.

He took her in his arms and kissed her and all her doubts

and arguments vanished with the touch of his lips and with his arms around her.

Bob said nothing to his father about the offer Mr. Hardesty had made him. The only thing that hindered him from taking the job at once was that he knew how it would hurt his father. He knew that his father was grooming him to take over the business when he should retire.

He knew that it was his interest in Jessie that had caused Mr. Hardesty to make the offer. The man knew that his daughter was in love with Bob, for she had told him so. He wanted the best for her, if she should marry Bob, and that was what had inspired him to make Bob the offer.

Bob knew that if he accepted the offer, which he wanted to do, it would precipitate affairs at home and also with Babs, and, for reasons of his own, he didn't want that to happen just now. He was hoping that the future would take care of the situation and that his affairs would be straightened out without causing too much trouble for himself or for anyone concerned.

He had no idea how this could be done. He had gotten himself into trouble and he didn't know how he was to get out of it. He would have to think of some way.

In the meantime he could be happy in the love of Babs, for her beauty was something that he couldn't resist, and her love was something that not only satisfied his vanity, but gave him a real thrill, as her adoration had done when he was still a little fellow and didn't know the real meaning of love. He didn't want her to love anyone else, no matter what his real feelings toward her might be. That he was being supremely selfish and heartless where she was concerned, he didn't stop to think. If he had, he probably wouldn't have cared. With his supreme optimism, he was sure that everything would work out somehow. That was his motto, the principle upon which he lived. Little did he know how wrong he was and that tragedy would be the result of this same selfishness and carelessness of anyone's feelings but his own.

CHAPTER FOURTEEN

As THE TIME PASSED and Warren became used to the routine of his work, he began to realize that though his ambition had at last been fulfilled, there was no joy of achievement in it. All his younger life he had had that one aim, to sit on the bench where his grandfather had sat. Now he was there and there was no joy in the knowledge that he had attained his ambition. It was like reaching a mountain top and realizing that there were no more heights to climb, that there was no way but down.

He had decided some cases that were bitterly contested and had been made the center of controversy between the two rival papers, but when his final verdict had been given, he received acclaim from both papers. They could not argue against what he had done, for the facts in the trial had left no room for argument and Warren's wise handling of the case in his decision had proved his wisdom and sense of justice.

He knew that he would be a candidate for the position in the next election, if he chose to run, and he felt sure that he would be elected and that he would likely hold the position for many years, as his predecessor had done.

The question in his mind which loomed larger as time passed, was whether he would accept the nomination or not.

His mother noticed his preoccupation and she saw that he was not as happy as he had seemed when he was first appointed. There were many times when she caught him off guard and observed a somberness about him which was not like him at all. He had always been so full of fun and so cheerful that it made her wonder what had happened to make the change in him. Finally she couldn't help but ask him about it.

"Is there anything wrong, son?" she asked as he sat alone with a book in his hands. He wasn't looking at the book, but was staring into space and the expression on his face was serious and rather sad.

He came to himself suddenly, unaware that she had been watching him and he gave her a smile.

"Nothing seriously wrong, little mother," he assured her. "I was just taking stock of myself and wondering what I should do about my future."

"Why are you wondering?" she asked in surprise. "I thought everything was settled, that if they offered you the nomination, you would accept the offer. I'm sure they will offer it to you."

"That's what I've been trying to decide," he told her. "I'm not so sure that I want to run for the office."

"Why, son!" she exclaimed. "Why would you want to refuse? You have achieved your ambition and in this little time since you've been judge, you've done such a wonderful work and the papers have commented upon it so favorably that we've all been proud of you. I think you've been wonderful."

"Thanks, Mom," and he took her hand as she sat beside him. "No matter if I was a complete failure, you would think me wonderful. Your love would overlook all my shortcomings. What would I do without you?"

"But why are you so undecided about running for election? I was sure that you wanted to run."

"It's hard to explain," he said gravely. "I've been thinking what a futile thing worldly ambition is, how empty when it is at last achieved. Perhaps I've made a grave mistake in making this my life's ambition. Now that I've attained it, it seems so empty. What glory is there in sitting day after day, judging criminals or else acquitting those who were innocent? Somehow I feel that I've missed something greater while striving for this little worldly place of honor."

"I don't see why you feel that way," she argued. "You're doing your utmost to render the right decisions and there are so few really honest politicians. Even those who sit as judges are not always acting in good faith. You are showing the people what a Christian judge can do. I think we need more Christians in political life."

"That's just the point, Mom. It seems to me that Christians are called for just one purpose, to win souls, or to witness to sinners, at least. I know we need men in politics who are honest and who have unselfish motives, but I'm wondering if the Christian should make politics his life work as I have done. All my life I've kept my grandfather as my ideal and I've tried to follow in his footsteps. I wonder if I haven't chosen the wrong ideal for my life. Instead of looking forward to sitting on the bench as judge, perhaps I should have chosen something greater. Perhaps I should have looked to Livingstone or Moody as my ideal from the human standpoint. And I should have looked to Jesus Christ as my real ideal."

"But you have, son. You've been a Christian all your life and you're still acting like a Christian. What's wrong with that?"

"Nothing wrong perhaps, but I feel that I haven't chosen the best for my life, that perhaps I've missed the mark. Now that I've achieved my ambition, it's an empty honor. What is there for me further, to just go on deciding cases for the rest of my life? What am I doing for my Lord? If I had set my ambition on spiritual achievements instead of worldly honors, I would perhaps now be on the mission field, winning souls for the Lord. My highest ambition would be to win more and more, to tell the story of salvation to those who have never heard it before. My life would be rich in rewards and though the hardships might be great, I would still be climbing to greater heights in service for the Lord. As it is now, there is no greater height to climb."

"I never thought of it in that way," she said thoughtfully. "Perhaps I have been wrong in not encouraging you to do something for the Lord. All I thought of was that I loved you and you loved the Lord and I wanted you to have the thing you wanted most in life. Perhaps I forgot that there are things better and more worth while than earthly honors or achievements."

"Don't blame yourself, Mom. You've been the best mother a man ever had. You led me to the Lord and you've helped me to grow. Perhaps both of our eyes were blinded by the god of this world. Perhaps another Livingstone or Moody has been lost to the world because of this enemy of man," and he gave her a shadow of a smile.

"Here lately," he continued, "I've been feeling that perhaps it isn't too late for me to make some better use of my life than sitting as judge. There are many others who are even more able than I who can fill this place, if I'll only step down and let them run for office. I'm still young enough to be used in some capacity in the work of the Lord, if it is only in an executive position in some office on the field. I'd never be satisfied to remain here at home when there is such need for workers out there. I'm seriously considering offering myself to some missionary organization when my term expires. It may mean that I would have to go back to school and take Bible training, but I'm not too old for that. I feel such a yearning to do something for the Lord while there is still time in my life that I'm getting impatient for my time as judge to expire. The desire has grown on me until I just can't ignore it. I feel that if I don't act upon it, my whole life will be wasted. I've lost too much time already. Just think if I had gone to Bible school instead of law school, I would have been in the thick of things out there. Unless I yield to this impulse, I'll one day stand before the Lord empty-handed. How terrible that will be!"

"I feel so guilty," his mother sighed. "How I wish that I had seen this years ago. I could have directed your life into a different channel. I feel that I've failed, but I'm so glad, son, that the Lord has laid this upon your heart. I shall pray that He will lead you in the way that you should go. How proud I shall be if you are able to be used of Him to win souls! I'll feel that I'm forgiven for not teaching you the most important thing in life before you wasted so much time in finding out for yourself."

"Suppose we don't mention this to anyone," he suggested. "I wouldn't want any hint of my intentions to get out before I decide to tell the committee I don't want to accept the nomination. Don't even mention this to Dad. He might not understand, for his one ambition for me has been that I should be where I am now. He will see the wisdom of it when he has had a chance to think it over. I'm glad that he too is a Christian."

"I'm sure he will understand and agree with you," she assured him. "He is so proud of you. You are his idol. Both of us are so grieved about Bob and Babs. I still believe that if Bob would accept the Lord, she would follow him and do the same."

"Nothing excuses her from being so wilfully stubborn about

thinking of her soul," he said gravely. "She can never say that she didn't know the right way, for you taught her just as you did Bob and me. She is so much in love with Bob that her eyes are wilfully blinded to the truth about what she should do, regardless of what he does. I'm afraid that one day she will regret it."

"I do wish that Bob would fall in love with her," Mary remarked. "It would make me so happy, for then I wouldn't be losing them. As for you, I've given up hope for you. You're destined to become an old bachelor and how terrible that will be!"

"Not as terrible as you think," he said as he put an arm around her. "Perhaps that is all in the plan of the Lord. Perhaps I can best serve Him if I'm not encumbered with a wife and family."

"I don't believe it," she argued. "God said it wasn't good for man to live alone."

"We won't argue about that. All I want now is to be in the Lord's will, to be what He wants of me and to be wholly surrendered to Him."

When they had parted, Warren sat for a long time poring over his Bible. Then he knelt and prayed. When at last he got into bed, he knew that if he could be accepted in any capacity in the work on the mission field, he would yield his life for service wherever and however the Lord would use him.

There was peace in his heart at last, peace that he had not had for a long time.

CHAPTER FIFTEEN

BABS WAS GETTING IMPATIENT to tell her mother about Bob and herself. Time was passing and they had made no plans, though Bob spoke vaguely of making some decision in the future. She asked him to let her tell her mother, but he urged her not to.

"Not yet," he explained. "I want to wait until I decide what to do about accepting Mr. Hardesty's offer. It's too good an opportunity to turn down without thinking it over. Until I decide what to do, we can't tell Mom and Dad."

"Why don't you ask Warren what he thinks about it?" she suggested. "He might be able to help you decide."

"I wouldn't ask him. I know what he would say. He would tell me that I was being disloyal to Dad if I left him just when he was teaching me the run of the business. He wouldn't be any help."

"Wouldn't that be the truth?" she asked. "Wouldn't you be disloyal and ungrateful to Dad if you walked out on him? He's counting on you to carry on the business when he retires."

"He won't be retiring for a long time yet," Bob argued. "Even if it does look ungrateful and disloyal, I must make my own decision, but it may take time."

He took her in his arms and kissed her and all her doubts vanished as they always did when she was in his arms.

"Just be patient," he urged. "Then we'll spring the news. There's plenty of time. Aren't you happy just as we are?"

"Of course I am," she said. "Just knowing that you love me is all I need to make me happy. Knowing that one day I'll belong to you is all I live for. I wouldn't want to live if you ever stopped loving me. But you've heard that so many times before."

He couldn't face the look in her eyes, so he let her go and left her.

Her eyes misted as she looked at his retreating figure. How handsome he was and how she loved him.

She knew that it would be like throwing a bomb into their crowd when they finally told the others that they were in love, for all of them believed that they were really brother and sister. She was impatient for that time to come, for she begrudged the attention that Bob paid to the other girls, especially to Jessie.

As the weeks passed, she was not only impatient, but a little bit worried. Bob was so vague about his plans and didn't seem inclined even to talk about them when she questioned him. She finally decided to do what she had always done, to take her problem to Warren. She knew that Bob wouldn't like it, but she was tired of waiting.

Warren was in his room after dinner and Bob had gone out upon some adventure with the boys.

"May I take up a little of your time, Judge?" she asked when she had been admitted.

"As much time as you want," he told her.

She came over to him and sat upon the arm of the big chair and leaned against his shoulder. He put his arm around her and smiled at her.

"Let's have it," he said. "I'm prepared to hear the case and to render a verdict."

"I have a problem. It's about Bob," she explained.

"Haven't your problems usually been about him? What is it this time?"

"I don't think he's playing fair with me. In the beginning, he didn't want to tell anyone about us. He was sorry I had told you. He said he wanted to wait until he decided about some plan that he had in mind."

"What was his plan?" he asked as a little frown puckered his brow.

"I can't tell you that," she said. "That is his problem. I suppose when the time comes, he'll tell you all about it. But right now I'm worried about us. I'm getting tired of waiting. It looks as if he's not willing for Mom and Dad to know about us. I don't know why, but I have a feeling that there is some other reason than the one he gave me. He talks vaguely about our plans, but he has never really come right out and asked me to marry him. Don't you think he should? If we're really engaged, don't you think he should give me a ring so that I can be like other engaged girls? I feel like I'm hanging on a limb that may break any moment and let me down with a crash."

"If he wants to keep your love a secret for reasons of his own, he wouldn't want you to wear his ring, for that would be a giveaway," Warren suggested.

"I never thought of that," she admitted. "I was just so impatient for him to let me at least tell Mom and Dad. I know it would make them happy."

"I'll speak to Bob," he said. "Perhaps he'll tell me what this mysterious problem is that he has to settle before the big secret is permitted to be out."

"Please don't let him know that I've talked to you," she urged. "He'd be angry with me and I couldn't stand that."

"You should be used to that after all these years," he told her as he gave her a smile and his arm tightened around her. "I'd not be able to remember the times you've come to me when you've been hurt by the boy. I do hope that when you're married, you won't have to come to me with that problem."

"I have been an awful nuisance," she said as she slipped from his embrace and stood up. "Perhaps when I'm married to him, I'll be able to brush off his hurts if there are any, but I'm hoping that there won't be any."

"So am I, little one," he said, patting her hand as it rested upon the arm of his chair.

"Thanks, big brother," she said and bent and kissed him upon his forehead. "As always, it's been a comfort to talk with you."

She waved to him at the door and left him. He sat there for a long time before he returned to his work. He wondered what this mysterious problem was that was keeping Bob from letting the world know about their love. He determined to find out what it was at the first opportunity.

It came a few days later. It was a Sunday afternoon. His parents had gone for a ride into the country and Babs was visiting in the neighborhood. Bob was taking a nap on the living room couch.

Warren wakened him and suggested that they should have a little talk.

"What about?" Bob asked belligerently.

"About you and Babs," Warren told him.

"What about us?" Bob persisted. "Has she been talking to you? I might have known she would. Well, I don't want to talk about us. That's our own little private affair. She shouldn't have told you about it. I wanted to keep it a secret for a while longer."

"Would you mind telling me why?" Warren asked.

"Yes, I would," Bob snapped. "I'm old enough to take care of my own affairs and I don't want any big brotherly advice from you. As for Babs, that's our own affair and no-body's business but ours."

"Have you never thought that perhaps you weren't treating Babs right by making her keep it a secret? She might feel that you're ashamed for people to know that you are in love with her. Why not give her a ring and let the public know that you two are engaged? That is, if you really are engaged."

Warren added this last seriously as his eyes bored into his brother's while Bob's eyes refused to meet his gaze.

"We're not really engaged," Bob finally burst out. "I've never asked her to marry me."

"Why haven't you?" Warren asked in surprise.

"Because I have no intention of marrying her," Bob told him.

"I don't understand," Warren remarked, stunned by this announcement and by the defiant expression upon Bob's face. "If you had no intention of marrying her, why did you tell her that you loved her?"

"I just sort of forgot myself," Bob explained haltingly. "She is so beautiful and I knew that she loved me. I thought it would make her happy if I told her that I loved her. I do, in a way, but not in the way she loves me. I'll never marry her, for I don't want her for my wife."

"Why not?" Warren persisted.

"Do you think that I'd marry a little guttersnipe, someone pulled out of that muck she was raised in, the daughter of a drunken no-good street-walker who died in the gutter?" His tone was more belligerent as he continued. "What would the world say if they knew who she was and where she came from? I'd be the laughing stock of all the crowd."

"You contemptible rat!" Warren cried furiously. "I don't have words enough to express what I think of you. How would anyone know about her past unless you told them? How did you ever find that out? No one was ever to know, least of all you."

"I heard Mom and Dad talking about it," Bob confessed.

"Why should it make any difference what her mother was? It's what she is now that counts and she's too good for you. Why did you lie to her and let her believe that you loved her and wanted to marry her?"

"I told you. She was so beautiful that I couldn't help it when I knew she loved me. She showed it in her every look and she all but told me in words. I thought it would make her happy for a while. I thought that after a while, she'd get tired of waiting or else she'd find someone else. I thought I'd get out of it someway or another."

"Just like you!" Warren blazed. "Thinking only of yourself and what you want. I suppose it didn't matter to you that it would break her heart when she found out that you had been lying to her all the time. You knew she'd never look at another boy. I'm ashamed that you're my brother."

"Thanks," Bob said with a short laugh.

"This is no laughing matter," Warren warned him. "What do you intend to do about her?"

"I don't intend to do anything," Bob said with a show of bravado. "I'm engaged to Jessie Hardesty. She has class and I'll be proud of her as my wife. We're keeping our engagement secret for the present. Her father has offered me a position in his firm."

"Are you going to let Babs go on thinking that you're in love with her until you announce your engagement to another girl?" Warren demanded.

"Isn't that as good a way as any?" Bob retorted. "I don't have the courage to tell her myself. You can tell her if you're so concerned about her. She'll fall in your arms and you can give her the comfort that only you can give, so she has told me so often."

"I have half a mind to beat you to a pulp," Warren declared.

"That wouldn't be a very nice headline for the papers," Bob retorted with a grin. "Judge beats brother to a pulp!"

"Get out of here before I do it!" Warren cried, white with anger. "You're not a man. You're a rat and I'm sorry that I'm your brother."

Bob turned to leave while Warren clenched his fists and struggled against the desire to really give him a beating.

Neither of them heard Babs' door close softly as Bob turned to leave.

CHAPTER SIXTEEN

Babs returned from her visit to the neighbor just as Warren began his talk with Bob. She had come in through the side door and walked softly down the hall, because she didn't want to wake Bob if he was still asleep. The door of the living room was open but Warren had his back to it and so he didn't see her slip by. She heard what they were saying, so she stopped and listened, unashamed that she was eavesdropping. She was so anxious to know whether or not Warren would persuade Bob to do the right thing about them.

What she heard stunned her. She stood there, petrified, and heard everything that they said, including Warren's wrathful words that ended their conversation. She went to her room and closed the door, then stood there leaning against it while her little dream world of happiness crashed in wreckage about her. Anger and humiliation swept over her, but grief and heartbreak crushed her so that she felt weak under the weight of it.

She dropped into a nearby chair while tears flowed down her cheek, tears of which she was unaware, tears of bitter humiliation and the agony of the loss of what she had carried in her heart for as long as she could remember. Bob, her idol from babyhood, was not the lover she had thought he was. He was just a cheat who had been playing along with her, satisfying his ego with her love and her beauty, and while he was pretending to be the lover, he was giving the love of his heart to someone else.

He was a cheat and a liar and he had made a fool of her. How he must have laughed at her while she was giving him

100

her lips and her adoration! How could he have done such a thing? She knew that he was selfish and self-centered, but that he should have gone so far was more than she could believe. Yet it was true. He had admitted it to Warren. Bitterness and hatred rose within her where love and hope and joy had so recently been, white-hot wrath that seemed to choke her, yet through it all, the tears continued to flow. She wanted to die, but she didn't have the courage to kill herself.

Life would have no meaning for her, for the one bright star of her life had suddenly vanished from her sky. As she struggled to compose herself, she began to think of her past life. It was a strange time to think of it, but pictures from the past flitted through her memory. She saw herself as a little tot, tagging after Bob, playing with Towser and so proud to be tolerated by Bob. She saw herself going to Warren when Bob hurt her, crying her heart out upon his knee and finding the comfort that she knew she would find, that she had always found through the years.

She remembered the time when Bob had first realized that she was no longer just a kid, but a young lady whom he admired and how she had thrilled at his first compliment of her beauty. The memory of his first kiss brought tears flowing faster but she ignored them as she sat there broken and crushed in a little heap.

Bob's bitter words rang in her ears when he told Warren that he never had any idea of marrying her, that he couldn't marry a guttersnipe. And her mother was a drunken no-good nobody, a street-walker. They had mercifully kept that from her. She thanked them in her heart, even in this hour of torture. She would have been a crushed, defeated child and her young life would have been blighted by that knowledge. But it was terrible to have the truth revealed in such a brutal way. It cut so deep that the scar would always be there.

Darkness began to creep into the room. She knew that before long they would be called into a Sunday night snack before church time. She knew that she could never face them now and she didn't ever want to see Bob again. She wanted to get as far away from him and the others as possible.

She got out a suitcase and began to pack it hurriedly. Then she went to her desk and wrote a note addressed to her mother. She sealed the envelope and put it there where it would be found by anyone entering the room. Then she slipped out the side door and into the gathering darkness.

Mary and her husband drove in a few minutes later and while Edwin went to his room, Mary went into the kitchen to prepare the meal. She was singing a little song and there was a smile upon her lips. She had had such a happy time with her husband.

When she had set the table, she wondered why the house was so quiet. At this hour, the children were usually on hand, hungry and talkative.

"Where is everyone?" she called as she came into the dining room. "Supper is ready. Come and get it," and she rang the little silver bell on the stand nearby.

Warren came out and joined them and when Mary saw his face, she knew that something was very wrong. She had never seen him look more serious and there was still an angry light in his eyes.

"What's the matter, Warren, and where are the others?" she asked.

"I don't know," he replied. "Bob went out sometime ago. I don't know where Babs is. She may have come in and taken a nap. I'll go and see if she's in her room."

He went to the door and knocked, then, as there was no answer, he opened the door and went inside. The room was dark and she wasn't there.

"She must still be out," he said when he returned to the dining room.

"That's strange," Mary commented. "She's always on time for her meals. We'll begin and perhaps those two will come in before long. Perhaps they went out for a ride together. I'm so happy to see them going together. Babs looks as if she's floating on air. It's wonderful, yet laughable, the way she worships Bob."

Warren said nothing. He had no appetite, but pretended to eat with relish. Mary knew as she watched him that there was something drastically wrong.

"What is it, son?" she asked. "There's something wrong, something very wrong, or you wouldn't look like that. You're scarcely eating a bite. What is it? Is it Bob?"

Some intuition told her. It had been Bob so often in the

past, in just little things, but now fear crept within her that this wasn't some little thing, but something really serious.

"Bob had better tell you when he comes home," he said. "I don't want to talk about it, so let's wait until he comes."

"I'm worried about Babs," Mary said. "I'll phone Mrs. Walker and ask her if Babs is still there."

She phoned the neighbor and came back to the table with a worried frown.

"She said that Babs left there three hours ago. Did Babs and Bob go out together?" she asked.

Warren told her that they hadn't. Something prompted him to return to Babs' room and turn on the light. He remembered having seen a little pile of clothes on the bed but he thought nothing of it. Now he wondered about it. As soon as he turned on the light he saw the note.

He gave it to his mother and she read it aloud.

"Dear Mom. I heard everything that Bob and Warren said about me this afternoon. If Warren wants to tell you, I think you'll understand why I'm leaving. I didn't know until this afternoon that I was just a 'guttersnipe' and that my mother was a drunken nobody who died in the gutter. I'm glad you didn't let me know, for all my life I would have been blighted by this horrible truth. You kept it from me in mercy. I wonder why I never quizzed you about my mother, but I'm glad I never did, for I was happy in my ignorance of what I am and what she was. I thought that Bob loved me, but I know now that he was only amusing himself with a little guttersnipe and making a fool of her while he was really in love with someone who has 'class and wealth,' whose mother is someone he can be proud of, not a drunken street-walker.

"I'm going away and I don't want any of you to try to find me, for if you do and bring me back by force, I'll leave again. I don't want anything to do any more with any of you, for I'm not fit to associate with you who have ancestors who lived clean lives. I've been made to feel that the sins of the mother surely do taint the child. As for Bob, I hope I'll find it in my heart to forgive him some day, for just now I hate him with all my heart. I'll always remember Warren and how I loved him, but now there is no place in my heart for even the love I had for him. I hate the whole world and wish that I was out of it.

"Let me warn you again not to look for me, because I'm not coming back, *ever*. I thank all of you for what you have done for me, a no-account little guttersnipe, and may the God you worship keep you. Just now I wonder if there is a God. Babs."

Mary read the letter with difficulty, for tears blinded her.

"What does this mean?" she asked in stricken tones.

Before Warren could answer the door opened and Bob came in. He stood a moment staring at them, for he saw the look of tragedy on their faces.

Warren turned to him and eyed him coldly.

"Bob can answer for himself. Let him," he said laconically.

Bob stood frozen to the spot and said nothing.

CHAPTER SEVENTEEN

As Bob continued to stand there staring at them, speech-less, Edwin spoke and there was wrath in his voice.

"Come in and sit down," he ordered.

Bob obeyed him, still saying nothing. He was afraid to ask any question, afraid to say anything.

"What does this note mean?" Edwin demanded as he took the note from Mary and held it up before Bob.

"How should I know?" Bob asked.

"This note is from Babs," his father informed him. "She has run away and you are to blame. Suppose you tell us just what happened this afternoon."

"I don't know what the note says," Bob replied in a des-perate effort to postpone the inevitable confession which he knew he would have to make.

"Perhaps this will enlighten you," Edwin said and he read the note while Bob listened with grave face and frightened eyes.

"Now perhaps you can tell us what this means," his father said.

Warren turned to him when he still didn't answer and said, "It's no use to play ignorant, Bob. As you heard, Babs heard our conversation and she's left home. You'd better tell them the whole truth. Don't force me to tell them. It's up to you."

"I can't," Bob stammered as he hung his head, for he couldn't meet their accusing eyes. "You tell them, please."

"Just like you to shift your responsibility to someone else," Warren said contemptuously. He turned to his parents and told them the whole story.

"Bob has been making love to Babs and leading her to believe that he really meant it. He made her promise to keep their love a secret. He had a reason for that. While he was leading poor little Babs on in a false hope, he was playing around with Jessie Hardesty. He claimed that Jessie's father had offered him a place in his business and he didn't want anything known about him and Babs until he had made up his mind about this offer. While Babs was waiting to tell the world about her happiness, Bob got himself engaged to Jessie. This afternoon I had a talk with Bob and he told me he had no intention of marrying Babs. All the other things he said about her you have read in the note. She heard everything and you know the rest."

Edwin turned to his son and there was fire in his eyes.

"You had better accept that offer from Hardesty," he blazed, "for you're no longer connected with me or my firm, as of now. If I did what I feel like doing, I'd disown you, but I still have the responsibility of being your father and of your poor lost soul. How could you do such a dastardly thing? It's unthinkable. Have you any idea what this will do to your mother, besides what it has done to Babs? What have you to say? Not that there can be any excuse for what you've done."

"I'm sorry. That's all I can say," Bob stammered. "I did care for Babs, but I just couldn't get away from Jessie. She was in love with me and she just kept after me. I couldn't turn her down. She had everything that Babs didn't have. I — I'm sorry," he floundered, then lapsed into silence.

"You're *sorry!*" his father thundered. "That's always been your excuse whenever you did something you knew was wrong before you did it. You were never sorry enough to keep from doing it, but only sorry that you had been caught and you knew that you would have to endure the consequences. Do you think that being sorry will change Babs' feelings and give her back her faith in mankind, give her back the joy she had here as our child? What do you think her future will be with this terrible scar on her life? Do you think that being sorry will ease your mother's heartache? Go on and marry this Jessie and may you have all the heartache that you've caused others," he finished bitterly.

Bob raised his head and met his father's eye as he said with a note of bravado, "We're already married."

"Oh Bob!" his mother cried brokenly. "How could you do this to Babs and to us?"

"Just like he has done everything else," his father said contemptuously. "He was thinking only of himself and what he wanted. How long have you been married?"

"Just a few days," Bob said. "We haven't told her parents yet. I was waiting until I could tell Babs."

"When did you plan to tell her?" Warren asked.

"I don't know," Bob answered lamely. "It was Jessie's idea, eloping the way we did. I didn't want to do it, but she insisted."

"Running true to form," his father remarked bitterly. "Blaming someone else for what you're responsible for. You didn't have to pretend to love Babs. I suppose you blame her for that. Since you're married to this girl, you'd better go and live in her home. I surely don't want you here. The sooner you leave, the happier we'll be."

"Oh no!" Mary cried in a heart-broken voice. "Don't send him away like this, Edwin! He's my baby and I love him, no matter what he's done. I'm still praying that one day he'll give his heart to the Lord. Don't send him away!"

"Don't worry, Mom," Bob said. "I'm going. I was hoping that I could tell you tonight. I didn't know that Babs would hear what we were saying and that all this would happen. I'll be all right. Don't worry about me."

He stood for a moment looking at them. He met his father's cold, angry eyes and saw his mother with her head between her hands as she wept. He couldn't look at Warren.

"I'll pack my things. I'll send for what I don't take with me."

He left the room and closed the door behind him. There was no sound but his mother's weeping.

Edwin put his arm around his wife and drew her to him.

"Don't cry, darling," he murmured. "Crying won't help. He's doing the only thing he can do. My heart is broken as well as yours, but I'm bitter against him for causing you to suffer. He's been a burden on your heart all his life. Only the

Lord can lift that burden. We'll have to keep on praying for him."

"I've almost lost faith in prayer," Mary sobbed. "I've prayed so long and so earnestly for him and for Babs and they seemed to get farther away from the Lord instead of coming to Him. In that Hardesty family, what chance will he have to know anything about God? They're so worldly and their wealth will be a temptation to Bob. His wife surely won't be a help to him."

"The Lord is still able, Mom," Warren said. "We won't give up praying and trusting. My heart is just as heavy as yours is, because of his shortcomings, but he was my little brother and I love him."

"What are we going to do about Babs?" Mary asked as she dried her eyes and tried to compose herself. "We'll have to find her."

"She told us not to try," Warren reminded her. "The only way we could begin to search for her would be to employ a detective and notify the police and that would bring the case into publicity. That would be worse than what has happened. It might unearth Babs' past and that would be disastrous. She would never be able to live that down. Just to know what her mother was has broken her heart. What would it do to her if she knew that the world knew?"

"But we can't let her go away and struggle for a living without trying to find her and persuade her to come home," Mary insisted. "I've lost both of them and it's more than I can take," and she began to sob again.

"You haven't lost her," Warren said, trying to comfort her. "She still loves us, even though she is so bitter just now. Give her time to get over this shock. I'm sure she'll want to come home when she has had time to get over the pain and disappointment. In the meantime, I'll do what I can to locate her without notifying the police. Let her alone for a while and pray that the Lord will work it all out according to His will."

"But what will she do to make a living?" Mary argued.

"She has a little bank account," Warren told her. "You and Dad have been most generous and she wasn't a spendthirft. Besides, if she runs out of money, she may want to return home where she had everything. Let's give her time and leave her in the hands of the Lord."

Edwin agreed with Warren, and Mary was forced to yield to their advice, though she didn't agree with them. She wanted to search for Babs and surround her with her love. She remembered the little lost waif who had come so readily into her arms in the long ago. Now she was out again, lost in a world that might drag her down before they could find her.

CHAPTER EIGHTEEN

WARREN TRIED TO ENCOURAGE HIS MOTHER with the assurance that things would work out with Babs as he had said they would, but he wasn't too sure in his own mind that they would. He knew how terribly Babs had been hurt. He knew how sensitive she was, how stubborn, and he was afraid that she wouldn't return.

What worried him most was the fact that Babs had no one to lean upon for comfort and strength in this time of trial and disillusionment. She didn't have the Lord. If she had Him, he felt that the Lord would sustain and comfort her from growing bitter and doing something that she might regret, but, since she had nothing but her own strength, he knew how little that would help her.

As the days passed and they heard nothing from her, he tried to trace her, though he knew that it was worse than looking for the proverbial needle in the haystack. He was sure that she had left town and he had no idea where she might have gone. He felt helpless and afraid for Babs, but the only thing he could do was to put her in the hands of the Lord. He didn't want to drag her into the limelight, for he knew that this would do more to hurt and humiliate her.

Mary had suggested getting a detective, but then she thought better of it. It might hurt Warren in his position, if it was known that his sister was a runaway. Warren told her that he wasn't thinking of himself, but of Babs. He knew that the longer she was away, the more difficult it would be to find her. So the days passed in anxiety and heartache.

Babs had no intention of returning home. In her state

of mind she felt forsaken by everyone and she doubted their love, even Warren's. She felt that they just pitied her, the little lost waif whose mother had died in the gutter, a drunken good-for-nothing.

The memory of that day when Warren had found her kept returning to her with a clarity she had not known before. She had seldom tried to remember that day and it had grown dim in her memory, but now it seemed only yesterday.

When she left the house, she took a bus that led toward the downtown area. In that section of the city there was a large shopping center, a number of restaurants, trailer courts, and motels. She rode on while she watched the signs on the motels to see if there were any vacancies. Finally she saw one and got off and engaged a room.

The next morning she went to the bank and drew out all her savings, then returned to the motel. She had spent an almost sleepless night. At first she was too stunned and bitter to shed tears, but as the night wore on, she became more acutely aware of her position and the tears came as she sobbed brokenly. The more aware she became of what she had done, the more heartbroken and miserable she became. She was already homesick for the home where she had known such happiness, but she felt that she had cut herself off from it forever. She wondered if Warren would try to find her, but when she remembered what she had written in that note, she thought that they might have taken her at her word and would not even look for her. She knew that Warren had no clue to her whereabouts, even if he should persist in trying to find her.

She began to take stock of herself and what she had done. She would have to get something to do. Her money wouldn't last long. She had no skill or training for any kind of work and she thought dismally that it would be hard to find anything that she could do.

She rode back to the shopping center and went from one store to another, asking for employment, but there was no opening. Where there might have been an opening, she was asked to give references and, since she had none, she was turned down. She was discouraged and she wondered if she would ever be able to find work. Finally she came to one of the cafeterias and asked for a job there. The manager asked her if she had any experience in serving at the steam tables and she told him that she had. It wasn't the truth, but that didn't matter to her. She had to have that job, for she felt that it was her only chance to get work. He agreed to take her on and told her what her salary would be. It was pitifully small, but it was better than nothing and she was relieved from any immediate worry.

She wondered how she would get along at the serving counter. She was terribly nervous and afraid that she would be clumsy and would betray the fact that she had never done that kind of work before.

She watched the girl next to her as the food was put out and decided that she would do her best to imitate her. The girl seemed friendly and Babs returned her smile with the hope that she wouldn't discover the truth about herself.

While Babs waited nervously for her first customer, the girl turned to her and said in low tones, "I know you've never done this kind of work before, so be careful and watch me."

Babs gave her a relieved smile and replied, "You're right and I'm scared stiff. I don't know what I'll do if I get fired. Thanks for offering to help me. Please do."

"You take the meats. They're already cut, so you won't have any trouble. I'll look after the potatoes and the other things here in this section."

Babs thanked her again and felt more confident. She was thankful that she had made one friend. She managed to get through the lunch hour without any mishap and she felt more sure of herself when they went off duty until the next meal. She turned to the girl beside her as they left the room.

"You surely have been a help and I do appreciate it," she told her. "I wonder if you could tell me where I could find a room that isn't too expensive."

"Don't you live here?" the girl asked.

"No, I don't," Babs told her. "I just came to town last night and I'm at a motel, but I can't stay there. It's too expensive."

"What's your name?" the girl asked. "I'm Ethel Horner."

"My name is Betty Lane," Babs lied glibly, giving her the first name that came to her with the same initials as her own name.

The girl looked at her speculatively for a while, as Babs wondered what was on her mind, then she said, "I have a little apartment over in that new section just behind here. There is only one bedroom, but if you'd care to share the place, you could sleep on the sofa bed. It would help us both."

"That would be wonderful," Babs exclaimed. "May I come there tonight?"

"Sure," Ethel agreed.

Babs felt relieved that she had found such an early solution to her problem. She had been too busy and under too much of a strain during the day to think about herself and her trouble, but when the day was over and she went back to the motel to get her clothes, everything came back to her and she felt the tears filling her eyes. What a dismal picture the future held. How different life would be, sleeping upon a sofa bed in a cramped little apartment. She thought of her lovely, comfortable room at home and pain filled her heart. She longed to take the first bus back and rush to Warren's arms and hear his words of comfort, to feel his tender caress and to know that he still loved her. But the thought of Bob and that she would have to live in the same house with him killed the longing.

She didn't sleep much that first night in her new home, even though she was so exhausted mentally and physically, and when morning came she felt washed out and disconsolate. The day loomed long and tiresome and uninteresting before her. She remembered that Bob and she were supposed to go on a boat ride with the crowd that evening. Pain tortured her and she found it difficult trying to appear cheerful as she and Ethel went to their work.

In the serving line there was a young man who stopped long enough to have a few words with Ethel. Babs couldn't help hearing what they said.

"How about tonight?" the young man asked.

"O.K." Ethel replied. "How about bringing Jerry? I have a friend living with me now. The girl next to me."

He took a swift look at Babs and gave Ethel a grin.

"That'll be easy," he remarked. "I'll be there at eight with Jerry. He'll get a big surprise."

When he had passed down the line, Babs turned to Ethel.

"I couldn't help hearing what you said," she explained. "Was that blind date meant for me?"

"Yes," Ethel told her. "You might as well go out and have

some fun. I'm sure you'll like Jerry. He's not a bad looking guy."

"But I don't want to go on a blind date," Babs objected indignantly.

"You can't sit at home and twiddle your thumbs every night," Ethel told her. "That's the only way you'll get to meet anyone. Why not try it? That's the way I met Dick. Come on and go with us. Jerry will be disappointed if you don't come. They're not tight with their money and you'll have a good time."

"I'll see," Babs conceded.

She didn't want to go on that blind date. But if she didn't go with this Jerry, Ethel wouldn't like it and she had been a friend to her when she needed a friend so desperately. Why shouldn't she go, she thought recklessly. She would at least have a time when she might be able to forget. It would be better than sitting alone and thinking of the past. She must try and forget that past.

Jerry and Dick proved to be entertaining at least. Though she found them rather crude and not at all like the boys she had been used to going with, they did their best to make them have a good time. They went to a show and then to have a late snack. The others took cocktails and had a drink with their meal and they teased her when she told them that she didn't drink.

"How come you don't drink?" Jerry asked.

"Drinks were never served in our house," Babs told him. "My mother was a sincere Christian and she taught me that liquor was harmful."

"Does your mother know where you are?" Jerry asked. "Ethel says you just came to town."

"My mother is dead," she said.

She was thinking of her real mother and her voice was bitter.

He mistook it for sorrow and murmured his sympathy, then dropped the subject, for which she was thankful.

"Now confess that you've had a good time," Ethel said when they were back in the apartment.

"At least I didn't have to sit here and twiddle my thumbs," Babs replied. "Jerry was very nice and he's not bad looking."

She was mentally comparing Jerry to Warren and Bob.

What a difference between the two of them and this new boy. She remembered Warren's clean-cut, handsome face and his polished manner and then she remembered Bob with his good looks and his genteel manner. These boys were crude and uneducated and they were ignorant of the finer things of life. She wondered where they got so much money to spend. The meal they had was lavish and expensive. They must have very good jobs to afford so much on one evening's entertainment.

Was this to be her pattern of life from now on, she wondered. What would these boys think of her if they knew the truth about her? They probably wouldn't care. But then, she didn't care what they might think of her and what she was, what her mother had been.

She wanted to be friends with them and if Jerry was to be the only means of her meeting others and if this was to be the life she would be forced to live, she might as well make the best of it. It was either that or to die of loneliness. In her present state of mind, she almost wished that she could die, for life seemed too great a burden to bear.

CHAPTER NINETEEN

A FEW NIGHTS LATER, the four of them went out together again. After that they went together frequently. Babs knew that Jerry seemed interested in her and she hoped that he wouldn't become annoying, for she was glad to go out and forget for a while. All she wanted was to have a gay time, so that when she returned to the apartment, she could drop off to sleep from sheer weariness and sleep dreamlessly.

She still wondered where the boys got all the money they spent so lavishly. When she asked Jerry about his work, he gave her a vague answer about being employed with some export firm. She wasn't interested in where they got their money, only curious. She enjoyed having them spend it upon her and that was all that she was concerned about, having a good time, no matter where it came from. Both of the boys had expensive cars and they used them alternately.

Babs knew that she was living recklessly and she knew that the kind of company she was with was not the kind that Mary would have approved, but she told herself bitterly that she was no longer subject to Mary's guidance. She was on her own now. She thought with a new sense of pain in her heart, that if Jerry should want to marry her, it wouldn't make any difference to him what her mother had been.

One evening Jerry came in a new car. Ethel was working late that night and Babs was feeling lonely. She dreaded to face the evening alone with her thoughts. When she answered the bell and saw him standing there, she was glad. It meant relief from boredom and the struggle to forget.

He said he came to show her his new car and to take her

for a ride in it. She hesitated, wondering whether she should go with him or not. They had never gone out alone together and there was something about Jerry that some inner voice warned against. He had never been anything but polite and friendly, but there was something that made her feel that she shouldn't trust him.

"Come on. What's holding you?" he asked. "I want you to see how this baby hits the road. I'll even let you drive it for a while."

She felt that it was silly to be so reluctant to go with him, so she got in and they drove off. They had not gone far when Jerry stopped at a corner and picked up another man, someone she had never seen before.

"Meet Steve Whaley," Jerry said. "You won't mind if he goes with us for a little way. I'll drop Steve off where he wants to see a man on business. Then we can go for a good long drive."

"Let's not go too far," she said. "Ethel will wonder what's happened to me."

"O.K., whatever you say," Jerry replied.

When they had driven further, Jerry offered to let her take the wheel.

"Let's see what kind of a driver you are," he remarked, as she slipped over and he went around and got in on the other side. "Take her out on the highway and then we'll drop Steve off. Open her up and see how fast she goes."

She put her foot on the accelerator and the car sped faster and faster. She felt exhilarated to be at the wheel again, for she hadn't driven for a long time. As they whizzed along, Jerry turned and nodded to Steve on the back seat, then he asked Babs to slow down and turn back toward town. She obeyed and finally they came to a warehouse and Jerry asked her to stop and curb the car.

"This is where Steve wants to meet his man," he explained. "You keep the motor running. I'll be out in a little while. See how fast she gets going when you give her the gas."

"There isn't anyone there," Babs said. "The place looks deserted."

She felt some inner warning that everything wasn't what it should be. She was beginning to be afraid.

"He's inside, in his office," Jerry told her. "Steve is supposed to see him about getting a job. He promised to wait here for Steve and see if he thought Steve could handle the job."

The explanation sounded pretty thin to Babs, but there was nothing she could do but accept Jerry's explanation and wait for him to return. They both went toward the building which was shrouded in darkness.

She saw Steve fit a key into the lock and her fears increased. If the man inside was expecting them, the door should have been open or else they should have knocked. She had half a mind to get out and go down to the main street and wait for a bus, but she decided that she had better stay where she was and wait for Jerry. Perhaps her fears and suspicions were groundless.

While she sat there waiting nervously for Jerry to return, a shot rang out from inside the building and the two men ran out while someone in the building fired more shots.

Babs saw Steve fall to the ground just outside the door and lie still. Jerry was running toward the car, but a bullet struck him and he staggered and leaned against the wall. Then he tried to run while the man inside came out and continued firing after him.

He darted around the corner of the building where there were some tall weeds and she couldn't see him in the darkness.

In a panic of fear, she put her foot on the accelerator and the car shot forward and sped down the street at top speed. Shots followed her and one of them struck the rear window.

She increased her speed and rode on in agony of fear and panic. She had no idea where she was going. Her one thought was to get away from that scene where she knew that an attempted robbery had been made. Presently she heard sirens behind her. She didn't realize that she was on the main highway and that she was exceeding the speed limit. She glanced back and saw two police cars following her. She knew that she would have to stop or be killed at the speed she was going, so she slowed down and pulled over to the side of the road as the cars came up and stopped beside her.

"Where do you think you were going?" one of the officers asked as he opened the door.

"I don't know!" she wailed. "I was just getting away."

"I'll say you were," the officer replied. "But you wouldn't

have gone far at that speed. You'd have gone into a ditch at the next turn and killed your fool self. Get out. You're under arrest."

"That's the girl," the other officer remarked as he came up. "It was a good thing that fellow could describe her when we picked him up."

"The other one was dead. So was the old night watchman," another officer said. "It was a good thing that he had someone there with him to help guard that shipment. That guy who was wounded will get the works."

"And you're in for your share," the officer near her told Babs.

"But I didn't do anything!" Babs cried. "I didn't know they were going to try to rob that place. I was afraid and I was only trying to get away."

"That's not what your boy friend said when we caught him," the officer told her. "You were driving the getaway car and you ran out on him. That bullet hole in the back of the car proves that you are lying."

"But I'm not!" Babs cried, terror stricken and bewildered. "He just told me that I could drive the car. He said they were going in to see a man about a job and that I should wait for them. I didn't know that they were planning to rob the place. Please believe me!"

"You can tell your story to the judge," the officer said as he pushed her toward one of the waiting cars.

"I don't suppose there's any need of putting the bracelets on her," he remarked as he opened the door for her to get in.

"Don't take any chances," the driver cautioned.

The officer took out his handcuffs and Babs had to submit to the humiliation of having them snapped on as she was put inside the car and the officer got in beside her.

"Good thing we had those two prowl cars on that beat," he remarked to the driver as they started off. "That other fellow seems to be pretty badly hurt. I feel sorry for the old man. He didn't have a chance."

"If the fellow lives, he'll get the chair," the driver remarked.

Babs began to cry softly as the tears streamed down her face. What an end to a life that had once held such promise of happiness! What could she do to make them believe that she had no knowledge of the attempted robbery? Every circumstance of evidence was against her. If she only had Warren now! How she needed him! If she could only go to his arms and find comfort from him. But Warren was a judge and the officer said she would have a chance to tell her story to the judge. *What if that judge was Warren?* The tears seemed to freeze upon her cheek. Would she have to stand before Warren? How terrible that would be, if she had to face him! She'd rather die.

They arrived at the prison at last and the car drove in under the gate and it closed behind them. Babs was taken to the women's division and the prison matron took her to the cell where she would spend the night in sleepless terror and despair.

CHAPTER TWENTY

WARREN WAS IN HIS OFFICE, looking over the docket for the day. He was depressed and his usual cheerful mood had sunk beneath the weight of sorrow and worry. He was sorry that he hadn't done what Mary had wanted him to do when Babs first left home, to put out a search for her. He was so sure that Babs would return when she had had time to get over the first grief and anger, that he had thought it best to leave her alone as she had told them to. He knew how she loved her home and how much she loved them and he was counting on that to bring her home.

When time passed and she didn't return, his anxiety and regret grew. He knew how lonesome and heartsick she must be and he was afraid that in that state of mind, she might do something desperate.

He knew how hopeless it might be to search for her now, but he decided that this was what he would have to do. He could no longer stand the strain of doing nothing and not knowing what had happened to her.

Home wasn't the same. When she and Bob were there, there was always chatter and noisy laughter, but now there was nothing but silence and a strained attempt at cheerfulness as they tried to carry on conversation. The conversation usually ended with Mary's question, "Do you think we'll ever hear from Babs?"

There would be tears or a brave attempt to hide them. Warren often felt like crying himself and he often paced the floor at night, until he went to bed weary enough to fall asleep. His dreams were so often filled with visions of Bab. When he wakened in the morning, she was upon his mind and in his heart, a constant source of pain.

Bob was out west with his bride and Warren was glad of that. Mr. Hardesty had sent Bob out to take a temporary position in the western branch of the firm. Bob was glad also, for he didn't want to have to face his family while his guilt was so strong within. It killed much of the anticipated joy of his marriage, for conscience was working and it gave him no peace. He couldn't help but think of what he had done to Babs and how his family felt, their disappointment and anger toward him.

Warren glanced over the docket again, trying to concentrate upon the cases that would come up this day. The first one on the list was that of a girl who had been brought in after being arrested when she was fleeing from the scene of a crime, an attempted robbery of a warehouse. There had been a murder and one of the robbers had been killed. The other was in the hospital with a bullet wound that might prove fatal. The girl had been driving the getaway car. She had pleaded not guilty, but the evidence was too strong against her and she had been indicted. She was to appear before him, so that he could hear her plea and set the date for the trial.

Warren read the name of the girl, Betty Lane. He uttered a sigh. Another young girl gone wrong. Crime was mounting and it seemed there was no way to stop it. Parents were so lax and so careless of their children when they were young enough to control. When they were old enough to rebel against parental authority, they drifted into crime and the parents tried to lay the blame upon anything or everything but themselves.

He disliked these cases more as time went on and he longed for the end of his term so that he could try to reclaim lives instead of condemning criminals. He would be glad when he could lay aside his judicial robe and never have to sit upon the bench again. He had already contacted a mission board and they were waiting for him to meet with them so that they could see just what could be done, whether he should go to Bible school or else go out on the field in the executive capacity for which he was already fitted.

He donned his robe and went out to wait for the girl to be brought in. His apathy vanished as he saw her walking down the aisle with the matron at her side. Her eyes were downcast and she felt weak and frightened. She had had a grilling ordeal before the grand jury and she had scarcely eaten since she had been brought in.

When she stopped before him, she raised her eyes and looked at him silently. Her face was white and her breath came in frightened gasps as she stood there, transfixed. She had wondered if it would be before Warren that she would be forced to face trial and she had hoped desperately that it wouldn't be he, but there he was, staring at her as if she were someone returned from the dead.

He said nothing, for he was speechless. He was trying to control his emotions, trying not to call her name out in agony as he had the wild impulse to do when he first recognized her. As she continued to look at him, feeling as if she were hypnotized, for she couldn't take her eyes off his face, she saw such compassion and such sorrow, such love, that she felt as if she would cry aloud.

They faced each other across the bridge of years past and memory stirred strongly within each of them. Babs wasn't looking at a serious-eyed judge with pain written upon every line of his face. She was seeing him as she sat upon his knee with her head upon his shoulder that was now covered by that black robe as if it were a shroud, a shroud where happiness and happy memories were buried. In memory he was looking down at the little girl when she first put her arms about his neck, while her dirty little face was so near his own and she had said, "Me like you. Do you like me?"

He was thinking of the years when she had sat within the fold of his arm and had poured out her woes to him and received the comfort that he was so willing to give. Now there was no comfort that he could give, only the cold dead words of the law. His heart was torn with grief and pity. Hers was torn with grief and regret and terror of what was to come.

Warren spoke and his voice seemed dead and cold to her. It was the voice of the judge, not the man she had always loved and from whom she had always sought and found comfort.

"State your case. What is your plea, guilty or not guilty?" he asked in his most official voice.

"I'm not guilty! I'm not guilty!" she cried hysterically, then she began to sob aloud with uncontrolled tears.

Warren was silent a moment. He knew that he could never sit in judgment over her, yet he was in a most difficult position. He was almost glad that she had become hysterical, for it gave him the excuse that he needed.

"Take the prisoner to my office and keep her there until she has become more calm," he said. "I'll let you know when I want her case continued. Bring in the next case."

Babs was led to Warren's office and the next case on the list was brought in. He went through the trial like an automaton, for he could scarcely think clearly. When that case was finished, it was almost noon and he ordered a recess until the afternoon session.

When he entered his office he saw Babs sitting slumped in the big chair beside his desk. An officer stood nearby. He told the officer to wait outside until he had finished talking with the prisoner, then he turned to Babs.

"Now tell me just what happened," he said. His voice was calmly judicial.

She raised her eyes to him and tears dimmed them.

"I know you must despise me," she said in a quavering voice. "What's the use of my telling you anything?" Her voice was bitter. "I've already been pronounced guilty."

"That was only the preliminary hearing," he told her. "All the facts and evidence will be brought out in your trial. I must know the facts and the truth from you before I can help you."

"Must I stand trial before you?" she asked as her tear-filled eyes looked into his.

"No," he told her. "You know I could never do that. Now tell me just what happened."

She told him the whole story as it had happened, how she had heard the shots and saw the two men fall and then Jerry running away. How she became panicky and fled from the place.

"This fellow is in the hospital," Warren said as he reviewed the case. "He claims that you knew all along that they were going to rob that warehouse and that you agreed to drive the getaway car. It was a stolen car, incidentally. This fellow, Jerry, has been a member of a stolen car gang and the police have been trying to locate the leader for some time. The one who was killed was the leader. This wounded

fellow accuses you bitterly. I'm afraid that his evidence will
be strong against you. I'll see what we can do, for I believe
you're innocent."

"Thank you," she murmured.

"Why did you run away, Babs?" he asked. "Did our love
mean so little to you that you couldn't depend upon us to
help you bear the pain and disappointment?"

"Why should you care for me when I was what I was?"
she asked in bitter tones.

"Don't you realize that Mom and Dad knew just what you
were when they adopted you? They loved you when you
were first brought home, all ragged and dirty. They loved
you then and so did I. We've loved you ever since, knowing
what you were and what your poor mother was. You threw it
all away when you ran away and doubted that love."

"I was so shocked that I couldn't think straight," she admitted. "I was sorry when I had time to think more calmly,
but I just couldn't come home and face all of you after what
I had done. And there was Bob. I never want to see him
again."

"Bob is out in California. You wouldn't have to see him
if you didn't want to. But you still have our love, dear, all of
it. I've never changed and neither have Mom and Dad. They
want you to come home."

"But how can I come home if I'm going to prison?" she
asked as her voice broke and tears filled her eyes.

"I'm going to do my best to see that you won't have to
remain there long," he assured her. "I'll ask Judge Madison to
handle the case. I'll recuse myself. I'm afraid the world will
have to know the truth about you, though."

"I don't care what the world knows, just so I can come
back home if you and Mom and Dad still want me," she said
through her sobs.

"Of course we want you, little one," he said and he put
his hand upon her head and gave her a gentle pat. She
caught his hand and kissed it while her tears flowed.

"I've longed for you so often," she whispered as she held
his hand against her cheek. "Just help me, Warren, please.
I'll spend the rest of my life being grateful."

"I don't want your gratitude. I want your love, Babs
dear," he murmured.

"You've always had that," she said as she looked at him through tear-dimmed eyes. "Now you have it a thousand times more."

He knew that she didn't have the least idea of the kind of love he meant and he knew that it was best that she didn't. His heart ached for her, for he knew how dangerous her situation was.

He summoned the officer and told him to take her back to her cell. She stared at him through frightened eyes but said nothing.

"The case will be continued at a later date," he explained to the officer, then he turned to Babs and said, "You'll have to remain there until Judge Madison and I can decide what to do about your case."

Feeling that the end of everything had come, Babs followed the guard outside and went with the prison matron back to her cell.

When the door closed behind them, Warren sank into his chair and buried his head between his hands.

CHAPTER TWENTY-ONE

When Warren met with Judge Madison, he told the whole story. He knew that he would have to do this when he asked to be excused from the case. He knew also that it would mean publicity in the most melodramatic sense. The papers would be screaming the headlines that a sister of the popular Judge Lancaster was on trial in a robbery and murder case.

Warren asked the judge if he would have the time postponed until he could investigate the case and try to get some evidence that Babs was innocent. Bail was arranged for her and she was released in Warren's custody.

When they drove away from the prison together, it was a broken and contrite girl who rode beside him. She was on the verge of tears, but she didn't want to cry. She had done so much of that since her arrest that she felt completely washed out, but when she reached home and Mary met her at the door with open arms and a welcoming smile, she flew to those arms and began to sob convulsively.

"How can you take me back when I've brought disgrace upon all of you?" she sobbed. "I feel so ashamed that I'd run away again, if it wouldn't cause Warren more trouble. How can you want me?"

"Because we love you, dear," Mary said soothingly. "Why can't you believe that? If you had only believed that when you ran away, you never would have left."

"I know I shouldn't have been so foolish, but I was so torn apart that I wanted to die. Since I couldn't do that, I wanted to get away from everyone I had ever known. I know now how ungrateful I was. Please forgive me."

"Of course we forgive you, dear," Mary assured her, "but we can't undo what has happened. I just hope that Warren can do something to get you out of this."

"I know that I'm in terrible danger," Babs said. "If Jerry still swears that I knew all about that robbery, I'll be in for a term in prison, won't I?"

"Let's not talk about it," Mary urged. "Let's try to forget it for a little while and be happy, now that you're back here where you belong."

"I'll try," Babs said, "but I don't think I can forget that I might not be here long. How I wish I'd never left!" and her voice broke.

Warren decided that he would go to see Jerry. The youth was still in a critical condition from the wound in his chest. The doctor told Warren that he had little chance of recovery.

Warren decided that he would do what he had done once before. He would appeal to the boy's better nature, if there was any of that left, and try to persuade him to tell the truth about Babs.

His visit met with failure. Jerry was suffering and he was bitter. He refused to change his original story, that Babs knew everything.

"I'll stick to what I said when they brought me in," he said as his face contracted with pain. "That dirty little double-crosser ran out on us. If she hadn't run away with my car, I would have gotten away and I wouldn't have been shot the second time. I hope she gets the works."

"What good will that do you?" Warren asked. "You're sure to get the death penalty, if you live to go to trial, and the chances are that you'll never live that long. What good will it be to you to know before you die that you've ruined an innocent girl's life? It won't help you and it surely would help her if you told the truth and made it possible for her to be exonerated."

"It'll do me a lot of good, just lying here and thinking that she's getting what she deserves for running out on me," he retorted. "You might just as well go away and let me alone. This pain is killing me."

"You may be more right than you think about that,"

Warren told him. "That pain is likely to kill you. The doctor doesn't give much hope for your recovery. Have you thought nothing about your soul and eternity? Whether you believe God's Word or not, it will be a terrible thing if you go out into eternity without God's forgiveness for your sinful life."

"Dying will be easier than the chair," Jerry said defiantly, "so let me die in peace. If it's got to come, I'll take the easy way out. That girl can live on and suffer for the rest of her life. She'll never forget what she did to me."

"Dying isn't the easy way out, boy," Warren said seriously. "If you don't surrender your soul into God's keeping before you go out of this life, there is only one place for your poor lost soul, an endless eternity in hell. Whether you believe in hell or not, it's there and everyone who refuses to accept salvation that Christ paid for on the cross of Calvary, when He shed His blood for man's redemption, will spend eternity there. It would be easy for you to acknowledge that you need a Saviour and ask Him to forgive you and save your soul, so much easier than dying and going to a lost eternity. I'm not talking about the girl," Warren said earnestly. "Let's forget her and talk about yourself. Why not get right with God while there is still time? I'll pray with you, if you'll let me."

"As if your prayers would do me any good!" Jerry scoffed. "You're just trying to get me to say that that girl is innocent. I don't want your prayers and I don't care what becomes of me after I die. I had a good time while I was living, so if I go to hell, whose business is it? Go away and leave me alone. And send that nurse here. I want something to ease this pain."

"I'm sorry for you, fellow," Warren said sadly. "I wasn't trying to do anything but to help you to escape an eternity of suffering and regret."

He left the boy, knowing that he was turning from a soul that might soon be in a place of eternal punishment. He had done all he could and he had failed in both efforts, but he still had faith to believe that God would open up some way of escape for Babs.

The thought smote him that Babs had never yet yielded her life to the Lord. Perhaps she might need to go through further trial in order that she might come to the place where she would ask forgiveness and receive salvation. He couldn't understand her stubborn resistance to all of his efforts through the years. There was nothing that he could do but pray.

Since the chief witness against Babs was still too ill to appear in court, Judge Madison decided, after a talk with Warren, to postpone the case for a while longer. Jerry had signed a statement, confirming what he had told when he was first arrested, but Warren hoped that there would be some way out, even if that was introduced in the trial.

Meanwhile the papers had gotten hold of the facts and everyone knew the story. Babs' name was flaunted on the front page as a sister of the judge and reporters played up the story. Pressure was brought to bear on Judge Madison for an immediate trial. The hearing was set and she was brought to court to stand before the judge and repeat her plea of not guilty.

Warren took her to court and sat beside her when she was brought in. He had engaged a lawyer friend to defend her and the lawyer sat on the other side of Babs. She sat there crushed and humiliated and frightened.

When she was called, she got up slowly and almost stumbled toward the judge's stand, for she felt weak and dizzy. At her previous hearing there had been very few in court, but today it was packed.

The judge asked her the same question that Warren had asked her, but this time there were no hysterics. She answered as calmly as she could, "I'm not guilty."

Just as the judge prepared to open the case, a court attache came in and hurried down the aisle, waving an envelope. It was a most dramatic moment as the judge stared at the intruder, then waited for him to approach, while people craned their necks to see what was happening.

"What's the meaning of this?" the judge asked sternly.

"It's from the hospital," the fellow said. "The messenger who brought it said it was important and told me to get it to you at once."

The judge took the envelope and opened it, then read it while the people waited, breathless. When he had finished reading the contents, he looked at Warren and there was a smile upon his lips.

"This note produces evidence that will bring an end to this trial," he announced. Then he handed the note to the court clerk to read aloud.

The note was written by the nurse in attendance on Jerry and signed by two other witnesses.

"The patient, Jerry Brown, held for murder, has just died," the note read. "Before he died, he made a full statement. This is what he dictated. 'Tell the man who talked to me that I'm sorry I didn't listen to him when he talked to me about my soul. I'm sorry I didn't do what he asked me to do about letting him pray for me, but it's too late now. Tell him that Betty Lane is innocent. She didn't know anything about the robbery. She just got scared and ran off with the car. Tell her to forgive me and I hope God will forgive me, but it's too late now, I suppose, to hope for that.'"

As the clerk finished reading the note, he handed it back to the judge. The judge looked down at Babs. Tears were streaming down her face, but she stood there facing him, oblivious of the tears.

The judge gave her a kindly smile.

"The signature of these two witnesses and the signature of the nurse validates this confession beyond a doubt. The case against you is dimissed," he said.

She covered her face with her hands and stood there weeping quietly. Warren came forward and put an arm around her and led her from the room while the crowd murmured their joy at the conclusion of the case.

"Oh, thank you, thank you!" Babs cried and buried her face against Warren's shoulder as they drove home.

"Don't thank me. Thank God," Warren told her. "I can't help thinking about that poor fellow and his lost soul. How I wish that he had listened and been saved before it was too late. I'm thinking about you too, Babs dear. I fear that you may do what that young man did, put it off too long. There may come a time for you when it will be too late. Have you ever thought of that?"

"I don't want to think about it now," she said through her sobs. "I'm just glad to be free again."

"Some day you may wish you had thought about it," he replied sadly.

CHAPTER TWENTY-TWO

BABS DIDN'T SEEM LIKE THE SAME GIRL she was before she ran away and the change in her made Mary's heart ache. Before, she had been so full of the joy of life, always ready to laugh and eager to go places and have fun.

Now she was so depressed that she seldom spoke except when she had to. She seldom left the house, except to go to church with Mary because Mary asked her to. She hated the stares of the people she had to face when she went to church and was miserable until she could get back home again.

Warren knew that her former friends had dropped her and he was glad of that, for he knew that they were a bad influence for her. But he felt sorry for Babs in her loneliness. He was worried about her, for he knew that she was going through a period of self condemnation and he realized what she must be suffering. There was nothing he could do to help her, for he had tried that and had failed, but he could pray and hope that time would help her.

One evening Warren told them that the committee who had been responsible for his appointment had paid him a visit.

"I had to smile at their embarrassment," he said. "They were so nervous and apologetic when they began their little harangue. They were trying to tell me in the most polite terms that they were afraid that the recent happenings might work against me if I were to run in the coming election. They were afraid that it had caused me to lose much of my popularity."

"How could they use that trial as an excuse?" Edwin asked wrathfully. "They must have been looking for an excuse."

"I think they were," Warren told him. "I believe that

when they had me appointed, they were hoping to use me. They should have known better, but they found out their mistake after I had been appointed. I set their minds at ease by telling them that I had no desire to offer my name for election. I had hated to tell them this when I had thought that they had been counting on me, for I had tacitly agreed to their proposal to put me up for their candidate. I almost laughed at their relieved expressions when I told them that I didn't want to run."

While he was talking, Babs suddenly left the table and went to her room. Warren heard her door slam and he realized that what he said involved her.

"How stupid I've been!" he exclaimed. "I might have known how she might feel about this. She doesn't know that I'm glad to be out of this. She thinks she's been the cause of what happened. Excuse me, Mom. I'll go and talk to her."

As he reached her door he heard sobs and he went in without knocking. She was sitting in the arm chair, slumped in a tearful heap and sobbing as if her heart would break. He sat on the arm of her chair and put his arm around her while he drew her head to rest against his breast.

"Will you never stop those tears, little one?" he asked gently. "Don't you know that they can never change things? They only tear you to pieces. What's the trouble now?"

He knew what it was, but he wanted her to talk, so that she would stop crying.

"I've ruined your career," she sobbed. "I've not only brought disgrace to the family, but I've ruined you and I can't stand that," and the sobs increased.

"Stop crying and listen to me, Babs," he said in commanding tones. "You're wrong about everything and even if you were right, crying won't help. You haven't ruined my career at all. If that trial made those men on the committee want to let me go as their candidate, they were making it easy for me to get out of a position where I felt honor bound to continue in it. I have wanted for some time to tell them that I didn't want my name on their ticket, but I didn't know how I could. Now I have made them happy by letting them know that I didn't want to run and I'm happy to be out of that situation."

"Why don't you want to run?" she asked as she stopped crying and looked at him in surprise.

"That's a long story, so let's sit over there on the couch where we can be more comfortable."

"I talked this over with Mom," he said as he sat down beside her, "but I never mentioned it to Dad. I suppose Mom will tell him now. I've felt that I'm doing nothing for the Lord by sitting as judge. I've spent my life trying to fulfill a very worldly ambition and while there's no sin in that, it surely isn't the highest ambition for a Christian. I should be somewhere out in the world trying to do something to win souls, working where I can witness for my Lord.

"That should be the first aim for a Christian, but so few recognize this, or if they do, they don't do anything about it. I was one of those many. But when my term is over, and I'm thankful it soon will be, I'll be going somewhere where I can help give out the Gospel to those who have never heard it before. If I can't be accepted in any other capacity, I can work in some office and turn others loose who are needed on the field."

"Are you sure that I didn't have anything to do with this decision?" she asked doubtfully.

"Not a thing," he assured her. "I was thinking of it before you left home."

"Couldn't you work for the Lord here?" she asked as a worried light crept into her eyes. "Why would you have to go away?"

"The need there is so much greater than the need here. There are so many here who are willing to work here, but so few who are willing to take the hardships of work in heathen lands. I've wasted so much time that I'm anxious to get going and try to make up for all the wasted years."

"When will you be going?" she asked fearfully.

"I don't know. I've been in correspondence with a faith mission board who have their work in Africa. If I'm accepted, I'll be going there."

"Oh dear!" she wailed. "If you go away and leave me, what will I do? How can I live without you? I won't have anyone to lean on if you leave me. Don't go, Warren! Don't go!" she cried and she clung to him while the tears flowed again.

"You could yield your life to the Lord and follow me out there where you'll be needed even more than I shall be, for you're young enough to learn the language rapidly. After a term at Bible school, you would be fitted to come out there and join me. Then we'd be together until the Lord returns."

She shook her head vigorously and drew away from him.

"I couldn't do that," she said dully, while the tears ceased and she sat there with bowed head. "But my life will be so empty without you. I don't see how I can go on. I'll be so lonely."

"Some day you'll meet someone who will make you far happier than I have ever been able to do."

"If you mean that I'll fall in love with some other boy, just get that idea out of your head," she said tensely. "I don't have any room in my heart for that kind of love. Who would want to marry me, if I did fall in love? Have you forgotten what I am? I hate even the thought of falling in love with anyone."

He put his arm around her and drew her to him again.

"Babs dear, if you would only yield your life to the Lord, you would find that there is still room in your heart for love and you would realize that, as His child, you would be led to happiness through Him. Somewhere there is someone who will make you happy and He will lead you to that person."

"I don't want to talk about it," she said.

"Why is it that you will never listen to a word about the Lord? When you were just a little tike you were so interested in hearing stories about the Saviour. What has changed you and made you so stubbornly refuse even to listen to a word of pleading to accept Christ and know the joy of salvation?"

"I don't know," she confessed. "I wish that I could listen, but when you begin to talk to me about the Lord, something inside me just freezes up and I don't want to hear it."

"Some day you'll wish you had. I pray God it won't be too late," he said sadly.

"When will you know that you're leaving?" she said.

"It will be quite some time," he told her. "I'll have to wait until my term ends, then I'll have to go and have a session with the mission board. In the meantime, please try to be a little more cheerful. Let's enjoy the time we have together, won't you?"

"I'll try," she said, "but I know that when you're gone there won't be anything left for me to live for."

He wanted to tell her that, except for the sustaining power of the Lord and the urge to do something for Him, he would feel the same way. He longed to tell her what was in his heart, but he knew that it wasn't the time to tell her. He doubted that he ever would. He would carry the ache of that love with him all his life. He knew that the Lord would give him strength to bear the pain and the loneliness and that He would supply something greater than that to help him carry on.

CHAPTER TWENTY-THREE

BABS TRIED TO APPEAR MORE CHEERFUL, but she found it difficult to pretend something she didn't feel. The thought of Warren's coming departure to some foreign land was constantly with her. She kept thinking of how empty her life would be when he was gone. She couldn't picture herself living without his comforting presence.

Warren surmised how she felt and did his best to help her.

"Try not to be unhappy," he said. "Life still has happiness in store for you, I'm sure. Just try to look ahead to the future and believe that all these unhappy memories will be buried under more pleasant experiences that will come to you."

"How can I be happy looking ahead when you'll be so far away?" she asked gloomily. "I want to cry every time I think about it and I can't think of anything else but you leaving me."

"Did you think of that when you ran away from me?" he asked.

"That's unkind of you," she said, looking at him reproachfully. "I wasn't thinking sanely then. I just wanted to get away from everyone."

"But I haven't gone yet and I may never go," he told her. "Even if they decide to accept me and send me overseas, I'll still be here a while longer. In the meantime you may find someone who will make you forget all about me and my going."

"As if anyone could ever do that!" she cried.

She put her arms around him and put her cheek against his.

"You don't realize how much I love you," she murmured.

137

"You've made me so happy all these years. No one could ever take your place. I'll miss you every minute you're gone, every minute until I see you again."

In his heart he was saying, "You don't realize how much I love you, my darling, and I'll miss you and long for you every minute that I'm away from you."

One evening the telephone rang and when Mary answered it, she heard Bob's voice.

"Bob!" she cried. "How glad I am to hear you! Where are you? It's been so long since I've heard from you."

"I'm here in town," he said. "I'm sorry I didn't write more often, but I was so tied up with the work that I just kept putting it off. We just got in this afternoon. May I come around and see you?"

"Of course, son. Come right on over. We're all here and we'll be glad to see you."

"He's coming right over," she told them. "I hope that you will be kind to him," she said to Warren.

"Don't worry. I won't say anything that will hurt either of you," he assured her.

Mary turned to Babs.

"Will you meet him, dear? I know it will be hard, but do try, for my sake."

"I'd rather not," Babs said. "Please don't hold it against me because I don't feel like seeing him."

"Do what you think best," Mary said, but Babs knew that she was hurt.

When Bob came, Mary took him in her arms and held him there while he kissed her and she told him how glad she was to see him. He could sense a feeling of restraint on his father's part and with Warren, though they both greeted him cordially. He followed his mother to a seat nearby and faced the three of them.

"I was anxious to come to see you as soon as I could," he began, "because I wanted to tell you first of all what has happened to me and to Jessie and why we came back home. We hadn't been out there but a little while when we saw the ad of a big meeting by a famous evangelist and we decided to go for curiosity. When the meeting closed that night we both went down the aisle and accepted Christ as our Saviour.

Your prayers have been answered at last, Mom," he said and he gave her a smile.

"I wanted to write and tell you right away, but I wanted to be very sure that what we had done wasn't just done under the inspiration of that sermon. I wanted to be sure that it was real and lasting and now I know that it is. When I look back on my past life, I shudder to think of what a selfish, wayward sinner I was. When I think of what I did to Babs, I could tear my heart out if it would do any good, but I know that God has forgiven me though I'm so unworthy. I came here to ask for your forgiveness for the heartache I've caused you and Dad. Do you think Babs will ever forgive me?"

"I don't know, son. You hurt her so terribly and what happened after she ran away didn't help any. I can't blame her for feeling bitter. Perhaps time will help her to feel differently."

"The reason I came home was to tell you, Dad, how sorry I am that I was so ungrateful for all that you had done to help me get a start in life. I was sorry that I had let you down, but I'm glad that it happened the way it did, for if we had never gone out west, we may never have been saved. But I have resigned my position with Mr. Hardesty. I told him that if you would take me back, I would work for you, but that if you didn't, I'd go out and try to get another job somewhere else. Money and position aren't the most important things in life. I can see that now."

He looked at his father appealingly.

"Will you let me try again, Dad, or would you rather not trust me?"

Edwin's voice shook as he tried to steady it when he replied.

"Of course I'll trust you again, son, now that you've come to your senses. You'll never know how your mother and I have prayed and suffered for you, but all that is forgotten, now that our prayers have been answered."

"Thanks, Dad," and Bob's voice was none too steady. "I promise that I'll try never to let you down again."

"You must bring Jessie over to see us," Mary suggested.

"Thanks, Mom. I know she will appreciate your wanting to see her, but I wanted to come alone tonight." He turned to

Warren, who had remained silent, and said, "Can you forgive me for what I did, Warren?"

"If God forgave you, how can I refuse?" Warren said. "Of course I forgive you."

"Thanks, fellow," Bob murmured. "Where is Babs? I wanted to talk to her if she would let me."

"She's in her room," Mary said. "I don't know whether she will want to talk to you or not. She said she didn't."

"May I try?" he asked.

Mary told him that he might and he knocked on Babs' door. She had heard everything and was waiting for him. She let him in and he stood there for a moment looking at her shamefacedly.

"I don't know what to say, Babs," he began, "but I just want to tell you that I'd give anything in the world if I could undo the past and wipe out the wrong I did you. I don't ask you to forgive me, but please don't hate me. I've changed and I know how wicked and selfish I was. All I can do is to say that I'm terribly sorry. I didn't deserve the Lord's forgiveness, but I know that I have it. I hope that some day you can forgive me."

As she stood facing him, for she hadn't invited him to sit down, and listened to what he said, she realized that there was nothing in her heart for him, no love, no hatred, nothing. He was just someone she had known and who seemed like a stranger to her. She was so relieved to be free of that burden of hatred and the fear that she still loved him that there was no bitterness in her heart, only a great relief.

"I don't hate you," she said unsmilingly, "and I don't love you. I wonder if I ever really did. I adored you when I was a little kid and I now think that feeling just sort of grew up with me, a sort of habit that I couldn't get rid of. I'm glad to know that there is no feeling at all in my heart for you, neither love nor hate, just complete indifference. If that's forgiveness, call it what you please. What has happened can't be wiped out. I still remember what my mother was and the way it was revealed to me and what I am, the child of that mother. Perhaps that will remain in my memory like a scar, but there's no use discussing that. That's all I have to say. Take it or leave it, just as you please."

"I'll have to take it for the present," he said sadly. "I

can't blame you for how you feel toward me. I deserve worse than that. But I know this, that one day you will accept the Lord as your Saviour and then I know you will feel different about the whole affair. When you have His love in your heart, you will have comfort and peace and even love for your bitterest enemy, which I know I've been. I know that one day this will happen to you, for not only Mom and Dad and Warren have prayed for you for years as they prayed for me, but I have been praying for you, that not only you would forgive me, but that God would so fill your life with joy that you would be able to live down the memory of the past and what I have done to you. I know that this sounds strange, coming from me, when you have known how wild and reckless and selfish I was, but I'm different as can be, Babs. I'm really a new creature in Christ Jesus and I long to see you have the joy in Him that I now have. Thank you for letting me talk to you. And may God bless you. I can't forget what a terrible sinner I was and how I wronged you. Like David, I can say, my sin is ever before me."

"Thank you for coming," she said.

He left and she closed the door. She crossed to the window and looked out into the darkness. She felt that a great burden had been lifted and that she was somehow washed clean within. There was no love, but no hatred. There was still bitterness and hurt, but she could bear that. It was the other two emotions that bore her down under their weight.

She heard the outer door close and then there was another knock on her door. It was Warren. She went into his outstretched arms and laid her head on his breast while the tears flowed silently.

"It was good of you to let Bob talk to you," he murmured as he bent and kissed her tear-wet cheek. "You've gained a victory and I know it will help."

"I can say truthfully that there is no more hatred in my heart for him," she said. "I told Bob as much. Neither is there the slightest remnant of the love I had for him. As I look back upon it now, I wonder if I ever really loved him or if it was just a little girl's adoration that became a habit."

"No matter, if you are free of it. Now I know that you'll be able to find happiness again. I shall pray that you may find it and I have a feeling that God will answer that prayer, for I believe that He does hear and answer prayer. Bob's conversion is just an added proof of that."

"How can I be happy when you're gone?" she asked as she looked at him through her tears. "How can I be happy when my comforter is no longer near me?"

"I shall pray that you will find another Comforter, One who can give you more peace and joy than I ever could," he said.

"I don't want any other comforter. I just want you," she cried.

She raised her head and kissed him on his lips. He held her close and his lips answered her kiss, then he let her go and left her. His heart was pounding and in that heart was the prayer that if it was God's will, she would always be near him, not only that he could comfort her, but that she would bring the answer to the prayer of his life. He didn't know how this could ever be, but, as he told her, he knew that God did hear and answer prayer.

CHAPTER TWENTY-FOUR

WHEN WARREN LEFT HER, Babs sat for a long time, thinking. A revelation had come to her that left her overwhelmed. It had come to her when her lips had met Warren's in her impulsive kiss. She remembered that other time that now seemed so long ago, when their lips had met and he had kissed her so tenderly, yet so clingingly, and the strange feeling that had stirred within her. She had wondered about it then, but now she knew and the knowledge thrilled and excited her, yet left her bewildered.

She knew that she was in love with Warren, not as the little girl who had come to him for comfort, but with a love that was so different from the love she had had for Bob. She realized as she sat there that what she had felt for Bob was not really the deep overwhelming love that she had for Warren. It was, as she had told Warren, just the outgrowth of a habit which had grown up with her through the years when she had looked upon Bob as her idol. That idol had proved to have clay feet and the love which she thought she had for him had vanished completely.

She must have loved Warren for a long time without realizing just what her love really was. She was thrilled with the wonder of it. How marvelous it would be to live her life as his wife. How tender and thoughtful he would always be. How happy she would be with his love surrounding her.

She sighed, for she feared that this could never be. Warren could never love her in the way she loved him. He felt that he was so much older than she, for he had told her so many times how he felt about his age. He still looked upon her as

his little sister and she didn't want that at all. It would take
a miracle for him to love her in the way she wanted to be loved,
and she didn't believe in miracles.

Mary was so happy over the change in Bob that she went
around with a song upon her lips as she used to do before
tragedy had struck.

Warren seemed more cheerful than he had since Bob had
left. He too was thankful and happy that Bob had returned
and that he had come to himself and returned to work with
his father. His time as judge was drawing to a close. He
was glad that in a little while he would be free from what
had become an irksome task. Then something happened that
changed everything.

The prisoner whom Warren had sentenced to a long prison
term for dealing in narcotics had escaped from prison. He had
eluded all efforts of the police to locate him.

Warren remembered the fellow's threat, but he hoped
that his family had forgotten it, for he knew that they would
worry. He decided not to mention it to them, but the papers
carried the news and Babs was the first to see it.

"That's the man who threatened to get even with you,"
she said when she had read the news item. "He may try to
carry out that threat. You ought to have protection," she
told Warren.

"That's one thing a judge has to face," Warren told her.
"There's nothing that can be done but hope for the best. Perhaps he has forgotten his threat. What he is concerned about
now is keeping his freedom."

"I'm sure he hasn't forgotten it," Babs insisted. "I saw
the look on his face when they took him out and I'll never
forget it. I'm afraid for you, Warren. Can't something be done
to protect you?"

He smiled and nodded as he said, "I can pray that the
Lord will protect me. Nothing can touch me without His will."

Babs wished that she had as much faith as Warren had, for
she was sure that the fellow would try to harm Warren and she
wasn't too sure that God would protect him.

A week or so later, when her fears had subsided some-
what, the phone rang and someone from the hospital gave her
a message that brought a cry from her as she hung up. Mary

ran into the room and asked what had happened. She thought that Babs had been hurt.

"It's Warren!" Babs cried. "He's been shot and they want us to come at once. It's very serious."

Mary phoned her husband and she and Babs drove as fast as possible to the hospital. When they arrived, Warren had been taken to the emergency operating room. They waited anxiously for what seemed like ages, while Babs paced the floor nervously. While they were waiting Edwin came in, white-faced and anxious.

Then they were told that they might go in for a minute, just to see Warren, for he was still under the anaesthetic. They filed in one at a time and then left and waited outside for the others to go in. Babs was the last. In this crisis, she felt that the other two should be there first.

When she slipped into the room and saw Warren lying there so white and still, he looked as if he were already dead and she had to restrain herself to keep from throwing herself down by the bed and crying her heart out. He had never looked so dear and she longed to just put out her hand and touch him. He was so handsome, even though he was pale and lifeless. She couldn't keep back the tears and she stumbled from the room and found a refuge in Mary's arms. They stood there for a little while as their tears flowed and Edwin talked to the doctor.

The doctor said he couldn't tell just what Warren's condition was, for he didn't know the extent of the internal injuries caused by the bullet, but he repeated that the chances were not too good for his recovery.

"They caught the criminal and he's back behind bars," the doctor told them.

That was small comfort for them. That wouldn't bring Warren back.

"We must pray that he will live," Mary said through her tears.

Babs went to her room as soon as they reached home, while Mary made preparations to return to the hospital. She thought she would pray as Mary had suggested. That was all they could do. She would pray that if Warren couldn't get well, that the Lord would take her too, for she didn't want to live without him.

As she knelt there, trying to put her prayers into words, the appalling thought came to her that she had no right to expect that God would even hear her prayers. She remembered what Mary had told her when she had listened with such rapt attention to those Bible stories, that there was no promise in God's Word for a sinner except the promise of salvation and that a sinner had no right to expect God to answer any other prayer except for His forgiveness. She remembered the many times Warren had pleaded with her to yield her life to the Lord, how he had tried to convince her that she would find peace and joy and comfort that He alone could give. She had so often refused the pleading of the Spirit because she didn't want to give up the pleasures that she felt were so important. Then, later on in bitterness she had turned her back upon that pleading. Now she felt alone and adrift, without any source of comfort to sustain her in this hour of need. She felt so guilty because she had refused, during all the stubborn, rebellious years, even to consider that she was a sinner, a lost soul, and that she had refused to ask for the salvation that had been offered to her so many times. She felt cut off from God and condemned. She had no right to expect anything from Him.

Would God ever forgive her and give her the gift that had been refused by her so many times? Had she waited too long? She remembered how many times Warren had said that he prayed that she wouldn't wait until it was too late.

She began to pray in agony, not for Warren, but for herself. She confessed that she had been so willful and indifferent and she asked the Lord to forgive her and to save her, to have mercy on her for waiting so long to accept His pardon and His love.

"If it isn't too late, Lord, if it isn't too late!" she cried heartbrokenly over and over.

Mary heard her sobs and she came in and knelt beside her and put an arm around her.

"Do you think it's too late for God to forgive me?" Babs asked as Mary drew her closer.

"No, dear, I'm sure that it isn't too late. You've waited a long time, but we both need Him now and I know that He knows that you need Him as never before, when both of our hearts are so torn with grief."

"I've asked Him to forgive me and to save me, but I'm afraid that I'm not worthy of His forgiveness," Babs sobbed.

"None of us is worthy, dear," Mary told her. "But if you asked Him to forgive you, I know He did. You must believe that He did, for His Word says that without faith it is impossible to please Him. You must believe that when you asked for forgiveness you did all that you could and you must believe that God has kept His Word when He said, 'Him that cometh unto me I will in no wise cast out.'"

Mary prayed with her and when she finally left, Babs had the assurance that her sins were forgiven and that she had at last received salvation. She was ashamed, as she looked back upon her past, that she had persisted so long in refusing such a wonderful source of comfort and strength even in this little while since she had believed. Though there was agony in her heart, there was peace and a trust and faith such as she had never believed possible.

Mary wanted to remain at the hospital during the night, but the doctor and her husband persuaded her not to sap her strength by staying. They knew that she might need it later on. When she went the next morning, Babs wanted to go with her, but Mary urged her to wait until there was some change in Warren, for the better, she hoped and prayed.

There was no change in Warren's condition during the day. He was still unconscious, with rare lucid intervals which lasted for just a few moments. When she came home that night, she told Babs that the doctor had told her that if he didn't improve within the next twenty-four hours, there was little hope for his recovery. Medical science had done all that was possible. Mary knew that it was now entirely in the hands of the Lord.

Babs went with her early the next morning. She asked Mary if she would let her have a little time with Warren alone, if the nurse would consent.

"If he's conscious even for a little moment, I want to tell him what has happened to me," she said.

"It will make him happy, if he can understand," Mary said while tears filled her eyes. "I tried to talk to him yesterday, but he never seemed to hear me."

The nurse gave Babs permission to be alone with Warren, but she warned Babs not to disturb him or try to make him talk.

Babs slipped to her knees by the bed and took one of Warren's lifeless hands in both of hers and put it against her cheek. Then she kissed it tenderly as she knelt there looking at his pale face. She put up her hand and stroked his brow and murmured his name. To her joy and surprise, he opened his eyes and a faint smile flitted across his lips. She knew that he recognized her.

"Oh, Warren darling," she murmured, "I wonder if you can understand what I want to tell you. They told me not to disturb you or make you talk, but what I have to say is so important. Please listen."

The smile returned to his lips and she believed that he understood.

"I want you to know that I've accepted the Lord Jesus Christ as my Saviour. Your prayers and Mom's have at last been answered."

His eyes opened wide and tears came into them and slipped down upon his cheek. A faint whisper that she could scarcely hear came from his pale lips. She managed to catch the words.

"Now I can die happy," then his eyes closed and he lay still.

For a moment she thought that he was dead and a faint cry escaped her, but she felt his feeble pulse and knew that he was still alive.

"There's something else that I must tell you, Warren, something that I want you to know before — before — if it is the Lord's will to take you home." Her voice broke, but she managed to continue. "I love you! I love you with all my heart. Not the kind of little girl love that I had for you, but the love of a girl for the one man in her life. Ever since I kissed you the other day, I've known it, but it must have been there in my heart long before that. I'd be the happiest girl in the world to be your wife if—if—you could live and if you loved me like I love you. Please, *please* don't leave me, Warren! Just get well and let me keep on loving you, even if you don't love me in the same way."

He opened his eyes and looked at her again and the feeble smile grew stronger. He made an effort to speak, but the words wouldn't come and he sank back into unconsciousness. Just then the nurse came in and whispered that she had better leave. She leaned over and kissed him gently upon his fore-head, then she slipped from the room. Tears were streaming down her face, but her eyes were shining through the tears.

"I don't believe that God will take him from me," she told Mary as she joined her in the hall.

"We must be willing to tell the Lord that His will must be done," Mary told her.

"I'll try, but it will be hard, for I want him so. Mom, I just told him how much I love him, not the kind of love I had for Bob, but something deeper and greater than anything I felt for Bob. I wanted him to know if—if—he had to go. I believe he understood."

Mary put an arm around her as they went down the hall.

"Did you tell him about your salvation?" Mary asked.

"Yes, and he whispered so low that I could scarcely hear him, 'Now I can die happy.'"

Mary refused to leave when night came. If Warren was to leave them, she wanted to be near him when the end came. The doctor said that there should be some change soon, for his strength seemed to be ebbing.

She sat quietly by the bedside through the long night hours, watching him and nodding when sleep overcame her. The nurse was there on duty, watching and waiting hopefully. Toward morning Warren stirred and opened his eyes. The nurse immediately bent over him and reached for his pulse.

He smiled at her and whispered, "I'm going to make it."

Mary heard and leaped to her feet and stood beside the bed. She didn't want to display any emotion, but she felt like shouting aloud for joy. Under her breath she murmured, "Thank You, Lord!"

When the doctor came in, Warren was completely con-scious.

"You surely have given me a bad time of it, fellow," the doctor said. "Thank God you're going to make it."

"I have thanked Him," Warren said in a voice that was much stronger.

Mary phoned the good news to Edwin and soon he and Babs were there. Mary met them in the hall and told them that they must stay only a few minutes, for Warren was still very weak and that he mustn't be allowed to talk much.

"I'll wait until Dad has gone in to see him," Babs said. "I won't stay long, but I want to talk with him alone."

"I understand," Mary told her and gave her a smile and a hug. "I believe I know what will happen."

Babs approached the bed diffidently. She was self-conscious, for she wondered if Warren had understood what she had told him. She hoped, now that he was going to get well, that he hadn't understood. When she saw the look he gave her as she stood beside the bed, she knew that he had heard and understood.

"Kiss me, Babs," he said.

She knelt beside the bed and their lips met in a lingering kiss.

"Did you really mean what you said about loving me?" he asked.

"Yes, I did," she admitted. "I thought you were going to die and I wanted you to know."

He smiled as he asked. "Now that I'm not going to die, do you still want me to know?"

"You already know," and she laughed a low laugh of sheer joy, just to know that he was going to live.

"When I heard that, I just couldn't die," he told her. He paused a moment for strength. "I wanted to live because the Lord had answered the prayer of my life. He couldn't answer that and then let me die."

"The prayer of your life?" she repeated, puzzled.

"That you would one day belong to me. I've loved you ever since the day I found you, but I never thought you would love me."

"But what about that other girl, that secret love of yours?" she asked.

His smile broadened and a mischievous light crept into his eyes.

"She just proposed to me a little while ago. It was you all the time."

She bent over and kissed him again. Just then the nurse came in and suggested that she should come back later. She gave him a smile and whispered as she rose from her knees, "I suppose you'll hold that over me for the rest of my life."

* * * * *

They were in the living room one afternoon. Warren was recuperating slowly but surely and the family was rejoicing over answered prayer.

"Are you very sure that you want to share my life, Babs?" he asked. "I'm so much older than you and I have plans, as you know, that may mean privation for you if you share them with me."

"What do eleven years difference in our ages matter?" she asked. "They say that a woman ages faster than a man, so I'll catch up to you before long. I'm sure that I want to share your life with you, no matter what privation it may mean. All I ask is to be with you."

Mary came in just then and gave them a smile.

"What is your wish for us, Mom?" he asked.

"Just that you two shall be happy together," she said. "And I know that you shall be."

"That's all that anyone can ask of life," Warren said seriously, "to be in the will of the Lord and to have the love of someone to share life with you."

"How wonderful the Lord has been to this little waif," Babs murmured as tears filled her eyes.

Warren drew her to him and whispered, "How wonderful the Lord was to let me find you that day."

"I can say amen to that," Mary remarked as she left them.

Upon her lips there was a smile and in her heart there was a song. What more could she ask of God? Nothing, indeed nothing.